Inside the House of Glass

a novel of staying

Cameron Lane

Stone House Editions

2026

Inside the House of Glass
a novel of staying

© 2026 **Cameron Lane**

All rights reserved. No part of this book may be reproduced, stored in a retrieval system, or transmitted in any form or by any means — electronic, mechanical, photocopying, recording, or otherwise — without prior written permission from the publisher, except in the case of brief quotations used in reviews, articles, or scholarly analysis.

Published by
Stone House Editions
Stories of the Heart, the Spirit, and the Unknown

eBook ISBN: 979-8-9992336-3-9
Paperback ISBN: 979-8-9992336-7-7

For inquiries or permissions, visit:
cameronlanebooks.com

Printed in the United States of America and other locations worldwide.

Table of Contents

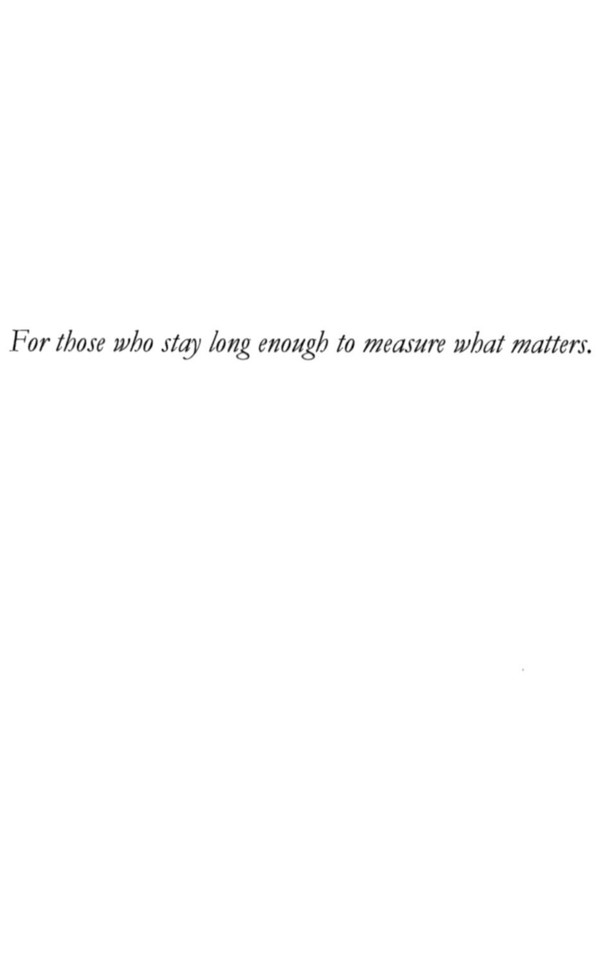

For those who stay long enough to measure what matters.

CHAPTER 1

The House of Glass

Steam clung to the mirror, his outline blurred into a ghost of himself. Zeb lingered there, towel idle in his hand, reluctant to wipe the glass clean. Behind the haze lay the face of a man who had fallen more times than he cared to count, and risen each time with something less intact.

Egypt, his most recent crossing, still pressed against him— streets crowded with voices that broke like surf, smoke coiling against minarets, soldiers' eyes flat and unreadable. He had walked among them as witness, not participant, carrying back a residue of dust that water could rinse from skin but not from the body's deeper memory.

At last he drew a circle into the fog with his palm.

The shape cleared only what his hand allowed. The rest of the glass remained opaque, unpersuaded. He could have wiped more—

could have revealed the whole face, every line earned and erased—
but he didn't. The mirror had already given what it was willing to
give.

He understood this kind of boundary.

Some surfaces reflected. Others contained. The mistake was
thinking either owed you truth.

He let the steam return.

His eyes stared back—steady, scarred, restless, as though some
river inside him refused stillness. Respect had carried him across
borders and into rooms bristling with suspicion. It had opened doors
that remained closed to louder men.

He dressed deliberately, each gesture a quiet vow. Shirt drawn
across his chest. Cuffs meeting the snap of polished links. The
familiar weight of his watch settling around his wrist. Not vanity—
armor. A discipline he trusted more than circumstance.

Clothing had never been performance for him. It was order
made visible, the line between chaos and composure. He dressed for
himself, for his own respect, perhaps for her glance. Never for the
world. That was her domain.

She dressed with the ease of someone accustomed to being
seen—lines and silks chosen for effect rather than comfort. He
admired her ease with it, sometimes envied the fluency of her beauty,
but mistrusted it all the same. Respect was his compass. Presentation
was hers. The difference was slight but decisive, and he felt it
tightening between them like a seam bound to split.

The hallway opened into light.

Glass walls framed the ocean, its surface scattered with fading
gold. The house was magnificent—too much so. Every line and
object gleamed as though chosen to be admired rather than used.

It was their house in name, but more hers in spirit: curated, impeccable. To him it felt fragile and gleaming, a house of glass where beauty carried a cost.

Beyond it, the ocean surged, untamed. Inside, silence polished itself to perfection—a silence that muffled more than it revealed. He moved through it like a guest, suspended between two selves: the man the world saw, and the one no room of glass could ever fully hold.

He paused midway down the hall, gaze drawn past the walls to where the horizon bled into evening. The sea stirred the memory of a river he carried within—unruly, ceaseless, always pressing forward. He had learned long ago that stillness was an illusion. Life was current, motion, the bruise and lift of water against stone.

Cairo's dust returned to him—the way it had gritted between his teeth, the way chants had risen like prayers only half believed. He had studied revolutions, their flare and falter, but this one had pressed its weight into ordinary bodies. That dust clung still, invisible but ineradicable.

And ahead—another continent waiting.

He would go, as he always did, not for spectacle or salvation, but because certain work did not tolerate delay. He carried scars into each journey: failed loves, abandoned work, ambitions burned to ash. Yet even scarred, the river carried him forward. Perhaps that was redemption—not triumph, not understanding, but endurance.

Goodness, he believed, outlasted brilliance. Respect could not be counterfeited. Even in places of suspicion, he had offered it, and sometimes it returned to him like an unexpected mercy. Yet here, inside a house, glass glittered like truth but offered only reflections.

At the corridor's end, the bedroom door stood ajar, warm light spilling across the floor. He slowed, knowing what awaited: a dinner arranged almost before his suitcase was unpacked, a return not only to her but to the atmosphere she carried with her. The measured conversation. The careful brightness. The version of himself she preferred to see. The masquerade was quieter tonight, but no less exacting.

Then she appeared in the doorway—silhouette framed in amber light, beauty so assured it needed no defense.

For a moment, everything else receded: Cairo's unrest, the ocean's pull, the house's silence, the questions that pressed at him from every direction.

Only her, standing there—radiant and unreachable.

He could have said more. He knew how.

He didn't.

His breath slipped. His voice softened, finding the one truth he did not have to perform.

"Hi," he said quietly. "You look beautiful."

CHAPTER 2

The Dinner Table

Vivienne chose the restaurant. It was the kind of place that did not announce itself. The name was short, understated, easy to miss on the street. Inside, the light was low but deliberate, arranged to soften edges and flatter surfaces. Conversation stayed just below volume, shaped by an understanding that presence here was meant to be felt rather than heard.

They arrived on time. Vivienne moved ahead of him as they entered, already oriented. The host looked up and recognized her before she spoke. A brief exchange followed—names, warmth, familiarity—her tone light, practiced. She did not ask about his evening. They were guided past occupied tables toward the back.

Zeb followed a step behind. His hands rested loosely at his sides. He noticed spacing, the choreography of servers moving without collision, the way coats were placed rather than draped. He registered these things without attaching value to them. They were facts, not signals.

Their table sat exactly where it should—quiet without being hidden, close enough to the room to feel included, far enough away to remain untouched. Vivienne approved immediately. She slipped out of her coat and extended it backward without looking. He stepped forward and took it, folding it once before placing it carefully on the empty chair beside him.

She spoke easily to the server, asking about the menu, about the sourcing of a particular ingredient. When the wine list appeared, she studied it with focus, not indulgence. She did not order for herself. She never did.

"This one," she said finally, tapping the page once. "He'll have that."

The server nodded and left.

Zeb did not comment. He rarely did. Vivienne's attention to detail—what he ate, what he drank, the quality of things that entered his body—came from care as much as control. He accepted it as part of the architecture of being with her.

When the wine arrived, Vivienne turned the bottle slightly, checking the label before the server set it down. She read it once, confirming the year, then nodded.

"That's right," she said.

Zeb watched the exchange. Accuracy mattered to her. Being mis-served was not an option.

The server poured a small amount for Zeb. He tasted it, nodded, and smiled faintly. "Thank you."

Vivienne did not drink. She folded her napkin across her lap, smoothed it once, and reclaimed the table.

Conversation unfolded easily. Vivienne talked about the week—people she'd seen, a gallery opening that had run long, a dinner she was hosting later in the month. Names surfaced and disappeared without weight. Zeb listened, occasionally asking a question, his attention steady, unforced.

When the food arrived, the server placed the plates down carefully, explaining one element of the dish. As she did, Vivienne listened with polite attention, chin angled slightly upward, her gaze hovering just above the woman's shoulder.

"Perfect," she said when the explanation finished. The word closed the exchange rather than opened it.

The server turned to Zeb.

He waited until she finished speaking, then said, "It looks great. Thank you for taking the time."

The phrase landed differently. Not louder. Just fuller.

The server paused—a fraction longer than required—then smiled, the expression arriving late, as if surprised by its own sincerity. "Of course," she said. "Enjoy."

Vivienne shifted slightly then, angling her body back toward the table, her hand resting flat beside her glass as if to close the space that had briefly opened.

As the server stepped away, Vivienne reached for her water and took a small sip. She adjusted her posture, crossing her legs, her body angling subtly back from the edge of the table. The movement was quiet but decisive, a reassertion of distance.

Zeb noticed.

Not with irritation. Not with judgment. With recognition. Recognition had become a habit with him.

The difference between them wasn't kindness. It was where it was allowed to land.

Vivienne resumed the conversation without pause, returning to a thought she had left unfinished. The room returned to its intended rhythm. Whatever relational residue had formed was sealed cleanly away.

They ate. Vivienne appreciated the food with discernment, commenting on balance, texture, restraint. Zeb enjoyed it without analysis. He thanked the server again when she refilled his glass. Each time, her response softened a degree, brief and human, before she moved on.

Vivienne did not watch this directly. She did not enter it.

Later, when the server returned to check on them, Vivienne answered first. Everything was excellent. Exactly as expected.

The server glanced at Zeb.

"It's very good," he said. "Thank you."

Again, that same pause. Unscripted.

Vivienne stood as the check arrived, already reaching for her bag. She signed quickly, precise, decisive.

Zeb waited until she turned toward the door. Then he folded a bill once and placed it beneath the edge of his plate, visible but unobtrusive. The motion was habitual, almost unconscious. Not generosity. Recognition.

Vivienne did not comment. She was already turning toward the exit.

They stepped out together into the night. The street was quieter than the room they'd left, the air carrying a faint trace of salt from the water nearby.

"Good choice," Zeb said after a moment.

Vivienne smiled. "I thought you'd like it."

He nodded. He did.

They walked on, side by side, their steps aligned.

Behind them, inside the restaurant, the table was cleared. The plate lifted. The folded bill discovered. The server paused for half a second longer than necessary, then moved on.

Zeb did not turn back.

Something had shifted.

Not enough to name. Enough to carry.

CHAPTER 3

After Dinner (Silences in Bed)

The drive home unfolded without friction. Streetlights passed in measured intervals, their glow sliding across the windshield and dissolving again. Vivienne kept the music low—something soft, curated to prevent the car from going fully quiet. She spoke once or twice, remarks that did not ask for answers: the way the room had filled, how well the evening had landed, how good it felt to be back.

Zeb answered when the spaces widened enough to invite him in. His voice remained steady. His hands rested loosely in his lap, palms open, as if he had already set something down.

At a red light, Vivienne lowered the visor mirror. The motion was reflexive. She checked the line of her mouth, adjusted a strand of hair, then closed it again. The light turned green. They moved on.

The house received them without resistance. Glass holding the ocean at bay. Silence already arranged. The air inside was cool and faintly scented—something clean, expensive, chosen to suggest calm rather than produce it.

Vivienne slipped off her shoes near the entry without looking down. Zeb picked them up and set them side by side on the mat, heels aligned. He hung his coat, smoothing the sleeve once before letting go. He watched her cross the living room and disappear into the hallway with the unthinking certainty of someone who never wondered whether she belonged.

In the bedroom, she moved with the same fluency she had carried all evening. Jewelry placed in a shallow dish. The dress eased from her shoulders and draped over the back of a chair, neither folded nor protected—care deferred, assumed. She paused briefly before the mirror, not admiring herself so much as checking alignment. Satisfied, she reached to dim the lights.

Zeb sat on the edge of the bed and loosened his cufflinks. He placed them together on the nightstand, parallel, deliberate. He removed his watch and set it beside them, face up. The ritual slowed him, anchored him in the body.

Amber light settled over the room. Beyond the glass, the ocean was no longer visible as surface, only as presence—dark, insistent, pressing without sound.

Vivienne slid beneath the sheet without speaking and turned onto her side. Zeb followed a moment later. He lay on his back first, letting the mattress receive his weight, listening to the house adjust around them: the soft intake of the air system, the near-silent correction of temperature, the mechanisms that preserved equilibrium without being asked.

Time loosened.

After a while—how long, he wasn't sure—he turned toward her.

She was facing the ceiling, eyes open, the light catching faintly on the whites.

He reached for her slowly, his hand settling first at her hip, then moving along her side with care, as if speed itself might bruise something. He kissed her shoulder. Her skin carried traces of perfume, softened by the evening's wine.

Vivienne did not pull away.

She did not turn toward him either.

When he kissed her neck, she released a single breath—controlled, measured—then tilted her head just enough to offer skin without offering attention. The distinction was subtle. It registered anyway, the way imbalance registers before a fall.

He paused. Not in protest. In recognition.

He moved closer, his chest against her back, his arm draped over her waist. He held her there without tightening his grip, without pressing. Presence offered. Nothing requested.

For a moment, her hand rested on his forearm. The touch was light, undecided. It could have meant warmth. It could have meant habit. Before he could tell which, her fingers slid away again, retreating to the edge of the sheet.

Her breathing slowed—not into sleep exactly, but into a quiet that resembled it. A stillness practiced enough to feel intentional.

Zeb stayed awake.

Or half-awake. Time began to blur at the edges. Thoughts loosened their grip and returned again without warning.

He listened to the ocean's pressure repeating itself in the dark. He listened to the house breathe—air cycling on and off, systems correcting imperceptibly. Reflections on the glass flattened into black.

He drifted, then surfaced.

A memory came without context: a narrow room years earlier, the smell of detergent clinging to his hands, the sound of a neighbor's television bleeding through the wall. He remembered standing at a sink, watching suds slide down porcelain, practicing stillness so no one would read his exhaustion as need.

The image dissolved.

Another surfaced—shorter, sharper. The sound of a zipper in the dark. The pause. A body turning away — not angry, not cruel. Simply elsewhere. No argument. No words. Just the space left behind.

He let it pass before it could settle.

Vivienne shifted beside him, drawing the sheet higher, the movement contained, economical. His hand still rested at her waist. He could feel her warmth. The outline of her body. The distance that remained untouched by contact.

He waited.

Sleep hovered, approached, retreated. Each time he thought he might slip under, awareness pulled him back—not sharply, just enough.

The quiet did not change.

He understood then—not as a realization, not as pain, but as something settling into place—that this was not the quiet he trusted.

Beneath it, the house continued its low mechanics—the faint cycling of air, a distant relay clicking somewhere behind the walls. Not silence, exactly. Maintenance.

He could have spoken. He could have asked if she was tired, if she wanted him, if something was wrong. The questions formed and unformed without leaving him. He knew how easily words could turn into requests, and how quickly requests could become performances.

So he stayed still.

He adjusted his arm slightly—not to hold her closer, only to remain there without pretense. He matched his breathing to hers, not because he believed it would reach her, but because it was the only honest rhythm available.

At some point—later, earlier, he couldn't tell—Vivienne turned her head a fraction toward him. Her eyes were closed now, lashes resting against her cheek. Her face was calm, untouched by effort.

Zeb watched her until watching itself began to feel like distance.

He rolled onto his back, leaving a narrow space between them that had not existed before. The mattress accepted the shift without sound. The house did not register it.

Outside, the ocean pressed and withdrew, unseen but audible now—the low drag of water against shoreline, the damp weight it left in the air.

Inside, the house held steady, unchanged.

CHAPTER 4

The Call of Elsewhere

Zeb woke before the light finished arriving. Not abruptly. There was no edge to it. His eyes opened as if they had been waiting for permission. The room held its shape from the night—glass darkened, air cool, the bed beside him still occupied but unmoving.

Vivienne slept on her side, facing away from him. The sheet rose and fell at her shoulder in a steady rhythm. Whatever distance had settled between them in the night remained intact, preserved. He did not study it. He did not measure it. He registered it the way one registers temperature upon waking—information, not alarm.

He slid his arm free carefully and sat up. The mattress barely responded. The house was built to absorb motion.

Bare feet touched the floor. The surface was cool, smooth, unyielding. He stood there for a moment, orienting himself in the quiet, then moved toward the hallway.

The house in the early morning was different. Without voices, without light performing itself, it felt stripped of intention. Objects remained where they had been placed, but without demand. The glass still framed the ocean, but nothing asked to be admired yet.

He filled a mug with water first, drank it slowly, then set it in the sink. He made coffee without ceremony—measured, automatic. No waiting. No pause for appreciation. He carried it with him toward the glass wall that faced the water.

Outside, the ocean was awake.

Not dramatic. Not still. The surface moved in long, patient intervals. Waves rose, folded, returned. The tide worked its way along the shore without emphasis, repeating itself without hurry. There was no sense of arrival or departure—only continuation.

Zeb stood with his weight evenly distributed, shoulders loose, coffee cooling slightly in his hand. He watched without narrowing his gaze, without searching for pattern. The pattern was already there.

Movement did not disturb the scene. It composed it.

The light shifted almost imperceptibly. The sky paled, not into color but into clarity. Edges sharpened. The glass no longer reflected the room behind him. It gave itself fully to what lay beyond.

He took a sip. The coffee was hot, unremarkable. It grounded him.

He thought—not in words, not in sequence—about the difference between holding still and being still. The house excelled at the first. Everything here was designed to suspend motion, to trap it in clean lines and reflective surfaces. Even silence was arranged, buffered, protected from interruption.

Outside, nothing was protected.

The water did not resist its own movement. It did not rush. It did not pause to announce itself. It simply kept going, pressing and retreating, shaped by forces that did not need permission.

Zeb felt his breathing settle into the same rhythm without effort. Inhale. Exhale. No attempt to match the sea. No need. The alignment came on its own.

Behind him, the house remained quiet. No footsteps. No doors opening. No sounds of waking. Vivienne slept on, held in the curated stillness she moved through so easily.

Here, alone at the glass, Zeb felt no urge to leave and no urge to stay.

The night had left its residue—not heaviness, not clarity, but awareness. He did not replay it. He did not ask anything of it. He let it sit where it had landed, the way silt settles at the bottom of moving water.

The tide turned again.

Not sharply. Just enough to notice.

He finished the coffee and set the mug on the counter without looking at it. Then he returned to the glass, hands resting lightly along its edge, watching the water repeat itself without concern for witness.

This was not peace.

The Call

The sound came quietly.

Not a ring. A vibration against the counter where his phone lay face down, muffled by stone. It was easy to miss. Zeb noticed it only because nothing else was happening.

He turned from the glass and crossed the room without urgency. The phone had stopped moving by the time he reached it. He picked it up, glanced at the screen.

A missed call. No name saved—just a number he recognized by shape more than memory. Below it, a message notification waited.

He did not open it immediately.

He carried the phone back to the glass and stood there again, the ocean still working itself into repetition beyond it. When he pressed play, the voice that filled the room was steady, clipped, practical.

There was no greeting worth keeping. No softening of edges. The message moved directly into information.

The situation had shifted. Not dramatically, but enough to matter. Timelines were compressing. Local partners were strained. Someone had pulled out. Another had overpromised. There were gaps now—logistical, ethical, human. Experience was needed. Familiarity with instability. Someone who could move without escalating, who understood what tension looked like before it broke.

The voice did not ask.

It assumed.

Zeb listened without interrupting, though there was nothing to interrupt. He leaned one shoulder lightly against the glass, weight settling, phone warm in his hand. The ocean did not change its rhythm.

When the message ended, the room returned to its earlier quiet.

He did not replay it.

He did not check the time.

He stood there for a moment longer than necessary, letting the information settle not into thought but into place. There was no surge of energy, no tightening in his chest. What came instead was something closer to relief—the easing that follows recognition.

This made sense.

He moved to the counter and opened his laptop. Not to respond, not yet. He pulled up a calendar, scanned the coming weeks. Obligations appeared and disappeared without friction. Some could be adjusted. Some would not matter. He noted dates without annotating them, then closed the screen again.

He returned to the glass once more. The light had strengthened, thinning the last of the night from the water's surface. The tide continued its work without regard for notice.

Africa did not enter his mind as a place.

It entered as weight.

Unfinished conversations. Arrangements left half-held. People who would absorb the consequences if attention failed to arrive. The work was not heroic. It was corrective. It required patience more than courage, restraint more than force.

He had been there before. Not often enough to claim ownership. Long enough to know better than to romanticize it.

There was nothing there that would save him.

Something there required him.

He felt no urge to tell anyone yet. No need to frame it as news. It could wait. The morning was still intact. Vivienne had not stirred. The house remained composed, holding its shape around absence as easily as presence.

Zeb set the phone back on the counter, screen dark, and rinsed the mug. The coffee had gone cold, unnoticed.

Outside, the water pressed forward again, unhurried.

Inside, clarity settled without announcement.

Movement as Clarity

Zeb dressed without ceremony.

A clean shirt, worn running shoes. Nothing chosen for effect. He moved through the bedroom quietly, not to avoid waking Vivienne so much as to preserve the morning as it was. She slept on, turned slightly toward the open space of the bed, her breathing steady, the sheet drawn neatly to her shoulder.

Outside, the island was already awake in its own way.

The air carried salt and coolness, the kind that lingered only at the edge of day. The light was still low, thinning rather than brightening, giving the ocean a muted sheen. Zeb stepped out and closed the door behind him. The sound vanished almost immediately.

He jogged down toward the water and turned north, following the curve of the shoreline. The sand was firm near the water's edge, packed smooth by the tide. His feet found their rhythm quickly, each step landing cleanly, the motion settling him deeper into his body.

The ocean moved beside him, close enough to hear, far enough to remain indifferent. Waves rose and folded without urgency, repeating themselves with patient consistency. Nothing here rushed. Nothing paused.

He ran without measuring distance. Without music. Without goal beyond the movement itself. His breath aligned naturally with the cadence of his stride, neither strained nor slack. The night's residue loosened and fell away without being examined.

Farther down the beach, a groundskeeper was already at work, raking debris left by the tide into neat, temporary lines. They exchanged a nod as Zeb passed. No words. No recognition required beyond presence.

At the far end of the island, Zeb slowed and turned back. The sun had not yet cleared the horizon, but the light had strengthened enough to sharpen edges. He ran the length again at an easier pace, then slowed to a walk as he reached the house.

Back inside, he showered quickly. Cool water. No lingering. He dressed again—simple clothes this time—and stepped out once more, heading inland along the path that led away from the houses.

The island's clubhouse sat about half a mile down, set back from the ocean and on the sound side, modest in scale despite its finish. Zeb walked there at an even pace, passing trimmed hedges, service paths, maintenance carts parked neatly out of sight. Workers moved through their routines without spectacle, preparing the island for the day it would soon perform.

Inside the clubhouse, the air was quiet and faintly cool. A few early risers sat scattered at tables, each absorbed in their own habits. Zeb poured himself a coffee, black, and carried it to a seat near the window.

He unfolded a newspaper—actual newsprint, creased and faintly inked. He liked the weight of it, the resistance of the pages. He scanned the headlines without urgency, reading some pieces fully, others not at all. The world moved at a different speed on paper. It always had.

No one interrupted him. No one needed anything from him here.

The movement of the morning had done its work. His body felt aligned, his attention settled. The house, the glass, the polished stillness they contained receded to their proper scale.

When he stood to leave, it wasn't because the calm had ended, but because it held.

He walked back toward the house along the same path, the island fully awake now, the day beginning to arrange itself around repetition and care.

Vivienne would still be asleep.

He returned without hurry, carrying with him the clarity that came not from thought, but from motion allowed to complete itself.

Vivienne Wakes

Vivienne woke into the morning as if it had been waiting for her.

She moved through the bedroom with unbroken composure, hair falling into place with only minor adjustment, skin already awake.

Whatever the night had held did not cling to her. She crossed to the bathroom, turned on the shower, and closed the door without comment.

Zeb heard the water begin, steady and confident. He remained where he was, standing near the window, the house resuming its preferred cadence now that it had company.

When she returned, dressed and luminous in a way that required no effort, she glanced at him as if taking inventory rather than seeking reassurance.

"You're up early," she said lightly.

He nodded once.

She moved into the kitchen, already speaking—appointments, a lunch she couldn't move, a call she needed to return. Her phone was in her hand now, screen lighting briefly, dimming again. She poured herself some coffee, leaned against the counter, checked the time.

The morning gathered around her quickly.

Zeb listened without interruption. When there was space, he said, evenly, "I heard from them this morning."

She looked up, interested but unanchored. "From where?"

He named it simply. No emphasis. No framing. "Things are shifting again. They may need me sooner than planned."

Vivienne smiled faintly, already processing the inconvenience more than the information. "That again?"

He did not respond. He did not need to.

She turned back to her coffee, stirred it once, glanced toward the glass. "You just got back," she added, not as protest, not as concern—more as observation. "You barely unpacked."

"It's not certain," he said. "Just movement."

She laughed quietly, a breath more than a sound. "You're always somewhere."

There was no edge to it. No accusation. It was said the way one comments on weather patterns—familiar, mildly amusing, beyond control.

She reached for her bag and began sorting through it, already half elsewhere. "We have dinner with Michael on Thursday," she said. "And the gallery thing on Saturday. Don't forget."

"I won't," Zeb said.

She leaned toward him briefly, brushed a kiss against his cheek, already turning away. The contact was affectionate, efficient.

"I'll be late," she added. "Don't wait for me for lunch."

Then she was gone—keys in hand, heels clicking once before the door closed behind her.

The house held the sound for a moment, then released it.

Zeb stood alone again, the air settling back into its polished quiet. What she had said replayed in him, not as words but as weight. Not disagreement. Not refusal.

Absence of gravity.

She had not opposed him. She had not questioned the work. She had simply absorbed the information at the scale it arrived— small, manageable, aesthetic.

He returned to the glass and watched the ocean continue its motion, unchanged by conversation.

The pattern was clearer now.

Not broken. Not condemned. Just visible.

Pattern Registers

After Vivienne left, the house returned to its preferred state.

The air smoothed itself. The glass resumed its work of holding the outside at a careful distance. Whatever traces of movement she had brought through—sound, warmth, intention—were absorbed quickly, leaving no residue.

Zeb did not move right away.

He stood where he was, coffee untouched now, watching the ocean beyond the glass. The tide had advanced again, lifting against the shoreline before withdrawing, unbothered by repetition. The motion was patient, unannounced. It did not accelerate. It did not stall.

Here, everything was arranged to pause.

Elsewhere, movement did not require permission.

He thought—not deliberately, not in sequence—about how often this pattern had already played itself out. Arrival followed by stillness. Stillness mistaken for rest. Then the pull outward, not as desire but as necessity. He returned. She departed. Or she remained, and he moved. The order shifted, but the rhythm did not.

The realization did not arrive with weight. It arrived with clarity.

Vivienne's world held together through continuation—events following one another, appearances maintained, schedules honored. Nothing in it demanded rupture. Nothing insisted on redirection. It was a world designed to remain intact.

His was not.

That difference had existed long before this house, before this morning. He had mistaken its quiet for alignment once. He would not make that mistake again.

Outside, the water turned again, reshaping itself along the shoreline without resistance. It did not fight the boundaries placed before it. It simply moved where it could, over and through, patient enough to endure.

Zeb rested his hands lightly against the glass, feeling the cool steadiness beneath his palms. He did not resent the house. He did not condemn it. He recognized its purpose.

Containment had its uses.

Current did not live there.

He stepped back from the window and crossed the room slowly, each movement unhurried. Nothing pressed him forward yet. Nothing needed to be named.

The day was still early.

Clarity had arrived without asking anything in return.

CHAPTER 5

The Fracture

By late afternoon, the house had shifted into readiness. It wasn't louder, exactly. It was fuller—of motion, of intention. Doors opened and closed with quiet efficiency. Voices carried briefly along the glass corridor and softened before they could linger. The temperature adjusted by a degree. Light settled into its warmer register, flattering without announcing itself.

Vivienne moved through it as if she were part of the design.

A tray appeared on the kitchen counter where there had been nothing minutes before. Flowers arrived and were set down, adjusted, rotated a fraction until the arrangement resolved itself. A staff member passed with linens folded over one arm, returned without them. No one waited for instruction. They moved in response to her presence, attuned to timing rather than command.

Vivienne did not supervise so much as circulate. She spoke in fragments—names, times, preferences—each one absorbed and carried away. Her energy sharpened as the house filled. She smiled more easily now, not because she was performing, but because this was the terrain where she felt most herself.

Zeb stood near the edge of the living room, a glass of water in his hand he hadn't touched. He watched the room assemble itself without interfering. His posture was relaxed, his attention steady. When someone approached him with a question, he answered. When a chair needed moving, he moved it. When Vivienne glanced his way and tilted her head, he followed.

She crossed to him and adjusted the collar of his shirt with two precise fingers.

"Stand straight," she said softly.

He did.

She stepped back, assessing him once, fingertips still at his collar. The gesture was intimate in the way a tailor's touch is intimate—about fit, not closeness. His father had done the same once, thumb and forefinger steady at his throat, adjusting cloth that would carry his name.

She nodded, satisfied, and moved on.

Guests began to arrive just as the sun dipped low enough to soften the glare on the glass. Vivienne received them with practiced ease. Names flowed easily from her. She kissed cheeks, laughed lightly, touched shoulders in passing. She asked questions she didn't need answers to and remembered details that made people feel held without being examined.

Zeb stood beside her without crowding her space. When introduced, he met eyes, shook hands, said the appropriate thing with calm precision. He did not withdraw, and he did not advance. He occupied the space allotted to him and made it comfortable.

A man with silver hair spoke to Zeb about renovations at the clubhouse. Zeb listened, nodded, offered a neutral observation. A woman asked where he had been. He said, "Away," and smiled faintly. She laughed, as if he'd been clever.

Vivienne turned briefly and placed her hand on Zeb's arm—one second of contact, light and unremarkable. To anyone watching, it read as affection. Then she removed it and continued speaking, already elsewhere.

Conversation settled into its proper volume. Music remained unobtrusive.

Zeb remained present within it, capable and quiet, moving when needed, still when not. He felt no friction, no urgency. The arrangement required nothing more from him than attention and courtesy.

Vivienne thrived. The more complex the evening became, the more fluid she grew. She threaded through the groups, anchoring conversations, smoothing transitions, carrying the room forward without visible effort.

The system worked.

Filtered

The first guests had settled into their places, drinks in hand, conversations finding their early rhythm. Vivienne stood near the kitchen island, listening to two people at once, nodding at one, smiling at the other, her attention distributed cleanly.

Zeb moved toward her when the space opened.

"There's someone I should check in with tomorrow," he said quietly, close enough that it didn't announce itself. "A friend from the docks. His father's been sick."

Vivienne turned toward him, her expression attentive but already adjusting.

"Tomorrow?" she asked. "We're supposed to meet the planner in the afternoon."

"I can go early," Zeb said. "It won't take long."

She nodded, not unkindly. "Just make sure you're back by two. They're impossible if you're late."

The conversation sealed shut.

A moment later, as she reached for her glass of water, Zeb added, almost as an afterthought, "I heard from one of the guys I worked with before. He's in town for a few days."

Vivienne tilted her head slightly, considering the information the way one considers weather.

"Well, that's nice," she said. "This week's going to be tight, though. Maybe next time."

She smiled once, quick and reassuring, and turned back to the couple waiting for her attention.

Zeb remained where he was for a second longer than necessary. Not because he expected more, but because he was registering the ease with which the exchange had resolved itself.

Later, as plates were cleared and replaced, Zeb found himself beside Vivienne again near the glass. The ocean had darkened to a deep blue; the glass reflected the room back at itself.

"I might need to head out for a bit next month," he said. "There's some work that may open up."

She didn't ask where. She didn't need to.

"How long?" she asked.

"Not sure yet," he said. "It depends."

Vivienne considered this. "We'll see what that does to the schedule," she said. "March is already full."

She reached for her phone, glanced at it, then slipped it back into her bag. "We can figure it out."

Figure it out meant adjust around it, if possible. Or wait until it passed.

The room filled again as someone raised a glass for a toast. Vivienne stepped forward easily, accepting the attention, offering a few words that landed warmly and moved the evening along. Zeb stood just behind her shoulder, present but unremarked.

As the night went on, he mentioned a name once more—someone he'd known for years, someone who worked with his hands, someone whose life ran on a different calendar. Vivienne acknowledged it with a nod and a smile that did not invite elaboration.

Nothing he said was dismissed.

Nothing he said stayed.

There was no resistance to push against. His world did not offend her. It simply failed to register as relevant to the one she was holding together.

Zeb felt the pattern assembling quietly.

Not as rejection. As filtration.

Vivienne's attention was not unkind. It was precise. It moved where it was needed and did not drift elsewhere. People, places, obligations that could not be integrated into the design remained outside it, untouched.

She was not choosing against him.

Zeb understood this as it happened. He did not press. Pressing would have required her to refuse, and refusal would have implied conflict. There was none.

He stayed where he was, useful, courteous, unremarkable in the way the room required. He answered questions when asked. He refilled a glass. He stepped aside when the flow of conversation needed room.

Vivienne moved past him once more and rested her hand briefly at the small of his back—a familiar signal, grounding him in the arrangement before continuing on.

To anyone watching, it was seamless.

And it was.

Repetition Assembles

The days that followed differed in detail but not in shape.

Vivienne's calendar filled quickly. Hosting folded into departure; departure gave way to preparation again. The motion carried itself forward without pause.

Zeb remained.

He was present when needed and unremarked when not. He returned to rooms already in motion and left them before they emptied. The pattern did not require him to interrupt it in order to participate.

Suitcases appeared in the dressing room, opened and packed with methodical ease. Clothes were laid out, folded, refined. She moved through these rituals without pause, already half elsewhere. When Zeb passed through the room, she spoke to him easily— requests, reminders, confirmations.

"You'll be here when they arrive," she said once, not as instruction but assumption.

"I will," he said.

And he was.

The house took on its familiar cadence. Guests came and went. Dinners concluded. Mornings reset themselves. Vivienne departed with the same elegance she brought to hosting—unencumbered, assured, already oriented toward the next room.

Zeb stayed behind.

He walked the island in the mornings. He read the paper at the clubhouse. He answered messages, returned calls, kept the days from collapsing into each other. The house felt different in her absence—not emptier, exactly, but paused, as if holding its breath.

When she returned, motion resumed.

She arrived with stories, plans, momentum. The house brightened around her, sound and activity returning to their intended levels. Zeb stepped back into place without comment, as if he had never left it.

This sequence repeated itself without announcement.

Return. Departure. Hosting. Absence.

Zeb noticed how often his arrival coincided with preparation, and how often her leaving aligned with his stillness.

The realization did not strike him.

It assembled.

I return. She departs. Always.

The thought arrived fully formed, without heat, without emphasis. It did not accuse. It did not wound. It simply named the rhythm that had been playing beneath everything else.

Vivienne was not leaving him. She was leaving from a place he occupied differently. Her world moved forward through momentum. His required presence.

Neither was wrong.

They did not align.

Zeb did not act on the recognition. He did not speak it aloud or test it against her. He allowed it to settle where it belonged, alongside other truths that did not require response.

The house continued its work. The ocean kept its distance. The pattern held.

And now, it was visible.

The Non-Conversation

It happened later, after the house had quieted again.

The last guests were gone. The staff moved through their closing routines with practiced discretion. Glasses were cleared. Lights softened. The rooms returned to their polished stillness, as if nothing had disturbed them.

Vivienne stood at the kitchen island, scrolling through her phone, one hip angled against the marble. She looked relaxed, unburdened. The evening had gone well. That mattered to her, and it showed.

Zeb dried his hands on a towel and set it aside. He moved slowly, not because he was tired, but because there was no reason to hurry.

For a moment, there was space.

Not silence exactly — more like an opening. A pause wide enough for something else to enter if invited.

Vivienne glanced up at him then, her expression open but uncurious. "You okay?" she asked lightly, already halfway back to whatever waited on the screen.

"Yes," Zeb said.

The word landed cleanly. Not defensive. Not reassuring. Simply true.

She nodded, satisfied, and set her phone down. "It was a good night," she said. "Everyone seemed happy."

"They did," he said.

She smiled at that, pleased, and reached for her water. The conversation had found its natural end.

Zeb leaned back against the counter opposite her. He could feel the shape of what he might say without forming it into words. He knew the language that would be required — careful, measured, reasonable. He also knew what would follow: explanation, clarification, negotiation.

He did not want any of that.

Vivienne waited a moment longer than necessary, as if allowing for continuation. When none came, she turned slightly away and began gathering the few things left out on the counter, stacking them neatly.

"You should get some sleep," she said. "Tomorrow's early."

He nodded.

They moved toward the bedroom together, side by side. She changed first, efficiently, slipping beneath the sheet without ceremony. Zeb followed, turning off the light, letting the dark settle.

She reached for him briefly, her hand finding his arm, a gesture of contact rather than inquiry. He held it there for a moment, then she let go and turned onto her side.

Her breathing slowed quickly.

Zeb lay awake beside her, not restless, not waiting. The non-conversation rested between them, intact and untroubled.

The opening had been there.

And it had closed.

CHAPTER 6

The Measure of Enough

Again, by the time the first guests arrived, the house no longer felt prepared. It felt inevitable. Movement threaded through the rooms with quiet precision. Staff appeared and disappeared along practiced routes. Nothing stalled. Nothing spilled over.

Music settled into the background, present enough to soften edges, never enough to lead. Light adjusted itself gradually as the sun lowered, the glass taking on a warmer register, the ocean beyond flattening into a steady plane of motion. Everything aligned without asking to be noticed.

Vivienne moved through it as if the house were extending her.

She did not direct so much as absorb and redirect. A glance shifted timing. A word—half a word—altered placement. She circulated rather than supervised, her presence calibrating the room's tempo as she passed. Conversations lifted when she entered, loosened when she moved on. She smiled easily now. Here, nothing needed explaining.

Guests arrived in combinations that suggested design rather than chance—people who spoke the language of rooms like this and did not need subtitles. Donors who understood discretion. Cultural figures accustomed to being received. People who recognized the language of rooms like this and spoke it without accent. They greeted one another with warmth that stopped short of intimacy, mirroring one another's ease.

Vivienne welcomed them as if she had been waiting only for this moment. Names landed cleanly. Details resurfaced without delay. She touched shoulders lightly in passing, laughed without lingering, held eye contact just long enough to confer recognition. People felt placed without being examined.

Zeb stood within the flow without interrupting it.

He stood where he had been placed and made the space steady. When introduced, he met eyes, shook hands, spoke plainly. When asked a question, he answered fully, without ornament. When conversation moved on, he let it go.

People listened when he spoke.

Not out of politeness alone. There was a steadiness to him that invited attention without demanding it. His voice carried weight without volume. He did not fill space. He settled into it. The room did not resist him. It simply did not require him.

He moved easily among guests, neither advancing nor withdrawing. There was no hunger in his posture, no need to be mirrored. He drank bourbon, outside the choreography of refills moving past him. When a chair needed moving, he moved it. When someone stepped aside, he acknowledged the gesture with a nod and continued on.

The room held both of them.

Vivienne read it horizontally—how conversations braided and separated, where density gathered, where it thinned. She tracked balance and optics, the sufficiency of what was being offered. When one corner grew heavy, she lightened it. When attention drifted, she anchored it elsewhere. The evening flowed because she kept it moving.

Zeb read the room vertically.

He noticed who lingered near the edges, who carried trays longer than necessary, whose movements tightened as the room filled. He registered strain where it surfaced briefly before being smoothed away. He saw what it cost for the room to float as it did, and how efficiently that cost was distributed.

A server passed behind him with a tray balanced carefully at shoulder height. Zeb stepped aside without breaking conversation, creating space without signaling the act. The server nodded once, already moving on. No one else registered the exchange.

Across the room, Vivienne laughed lightly at something someone had said, her attention already shifting to the next arrival. The room adjusted with her.

Glass reflected light and movement without distortion. The ocean remained present but contained, its scale reduced to backdrop.

This was the system at full expression.

And within it, two measures of enough coexisted—aligned in form, divergent in weight—without friction, without speech, without judgment.

Not yet.

The Labor Moment

It happened without announcing itself.

A brief tightening in the room—nothing anyone could have named afterward. A pause where movement hesitated just long enough to register as friction before smoothing again.

A server emerged from the kitchen carrying two trays instead of one. The weight shifted mid-step. Glasses trembled faintly, then steadied. The path through the room narrowed as guests leaned closer to one another, conversations uninterrupted.

Zeb noticed.

Not because it disrupted the evening, but because the rhythm changed. He angled his body slightly, opening space without leaving his conversation.

The server passed, shoulders tight.

One glass tilted—just enough for the rim to touch the tray's edge before settling.

Zeb reached out without thinking. Two fingers at the base. The tremor stopped.

"Got it," he said quietly—not to the room, not even really to the server. Just enough sound to register recognition.

The server met his eyes for an instant. Relief flickered there, quickly masked by professionalism. A nod followed—small, contained. Then the server moved on, trays balanced, path clear.

No one nearby reacted.

Conversation flowed over the moment without interruption. Laughter rose and fell. Music continued its low, steady presence. The room absorbed the correction as if nothing had occurred.

Across the space, Vivienne saw it.

Not the glass, not the tray—but the deviation. The slight change in rhythm. The way Zeb had stepped out of the choreography without disturbing it.

Her attention sharpened for half a beat.

She felt no embarrassment. No concern that something had gone wrong. The evening remained intact. The house was doing exactly what it had been designed to do.

What registered instead was irritation—faint, fleeting, quickly contained.

Not at Zeb's kindness.

At the way he could cross into that layer of the room without effort. The way recognition entered where she curated smoothness. The way a seam became visible—not torn, not exposed, but acknowledged.

She moved immediately.

Not toward Zeb. Toward the system.

A word to a staff member as she passed—quiet, precise. A shift in placement near the bar. Another server appeared moments later, redistributing trays, adjusting flow. The understaffed seam closed without comment.

The correction was seamless.

Professional. Discreet. Final.

By the time the next group of guests arrived, there was no trace of strain. Glasses refilled themselves. Servers moved with restored symmetry. The room returned fully to its intended register.

Zeb resumed his place in conversation as if he had never left it.

No one thanked him. No one needed to. The moment had not been for the room.

Vivienne crossed behind him a few minutes later, her hand resting briefly at his back—light contact, grounding, familiar. The gesture read as affection to anyone watching.

He did not turn.

The evening continued.

The system closed over the seam completely, leaving behind no evidence that it had ever existed—except in the body of the person who had carried the trays, now moving with slightly eased shoulders, and in the quiet recognition Zeb did not examine.

The house held.

The guests remained at ease.

Nothing had been interrupted.

The Van Gogh Moment

It came later, once the evening had settled into itself.

The house no longer adjusted. The rhythm held. Conversations had found their depth and their limits, flowing easily between groups that had already established their boundaries. Music softened further, receding until it functioned as texture rather than sound.

Zeb stood near the long table with a small group, a bourbon in his hand. The ocean beyond the glass had darkened to a uniform plane, its motion reduced to suggestion. Light inside the house carried the room now, reflections layering faces and gestures into a coherent whole.

Someone was speaking about the world beyond the island— markets shifting, elections approaching, places growing less predictable. The tone was measured, informed, abstracted just enough to remain comfortable.

Another voice followed, then another.

Then someone turned to Zeb.

"You've been around more than most of us," the man said, not unkindly. "What do you make of it?"

The question was casual. It did not ask for authority. It invited perspective.

Zeb did not answer immediately.

Not because he was searching for words, but because he was deciding how little was required. He set the glass down, resting it on the table without sound.

"When things get unstable," he said, "it's usually because the cost has been moving for a long time before anyone names it."

The group stilled.

He did not look around the room. He spoke to the space between them.

"Effort shifts first," he continued. "Who's carrying it. How much. How long. You don't see it from the places where things still work."

His voice was even. There was no emphasis, no invitation to be impressed.

"But it shows up eventually," he said. "Not as crisis at first. Just as strain. People adjusting without being asked. Making do. Absorbing what doesn't fit anymore."

No one interrupted.

Phones remained untouched. A woman leaned back slightly, her attention fixed. Someone nodded once, slowly, not in agreement so much as recognition.

Zeb did not elaborate.

"That's usually the measure," he said. "How much people are expected to absorb before it's noticed."

He stopped.

Silence held.

Not awkward. Not heavy. Simply present.

For a moment, gravity entered the room—without accusation, without demand. It settled briefly, like weight placed carefully on a surface that could bear it—but only briefly.

Then someone cleared their throat.

"That's true," another voice said lightly. "But it does seem like things have a way of correcting themselves."

A different man smiled. "And people are resilient," he added. "They always find a way."

The energy shifted almost imperceptibly. The words reframed what had been said, lifting it away from cost and returning it to reassurance.

Vivienne had been listening from a few steps away.

She stepped forward now, seamlessly entering the space Zeb's words had opened. Her smile was warm, unhurried.

"I think that's why evenings like this matter," she said. "People coming together, sharing ideas, staying connected. It reminds us what works."

She touched Zeb's arm briefly as she spoke—light, affectionate, grounding. The gesture read as unity, not interruption.

The group relaxed.

Someone laughed softly. Another reached for a glass. Conversation resumed, redirected toward travel plans, upcoming events, a restaurant opening that had been difficult to get into.

The moment passed.

Zeb remained where he was, his posture unchanged. He felt no disappointment. No irritation. He had not expected the room to hold what he had offered.

He had answered the question honestly. That was enough.

Across the room, Vivienne moved on, already engaged elsewhere, the evening continuing to respond to her with effortless precision.

Someone laughed softly. Another reached for a glass.

Beauty returned to its frame.

And without anyone naming it, the value was set.

Recognition Without Conflict

Zeb did not feel exposed by what he had said.

There was no recoil, no sense of having overstepped. The room had received his words exactly as offered—with attention, with courtesy, without resistance.

The room held it briefly—just long enough—then released it.

He understood this without disappointment. It had functioned as designed. His words had entered, rested briefly, then been set aside to allow the larger structure to continue unhindered.

Zeb felt no urge to retrieve them.

He moved with Vivienne through the remainder of the evening as he always did, their paths crossing and separating with practiced ease. When she returned to his side, he matched her pace. When she stepped ahead, he followed without lag. They spoke briefly—nothing of consequence, nothing requiring response.

She was luminous now, energized by the evening's momentum. Compliments found her easily and slid off just as easily, absorbed without altering her posture. She listened, smiled, redirected. The room continued to work because she continued to work it.

At one point, their eyes met across the space.

The look passed quickly—no message attached, no question posed. But something registered.

Vivienne felt it as a limit, not a loss.

Zeb carried a gravity she could not host. It required a different kind of room.

The awareness flickered and moved on.

The evening was intact. Her life was intact. The system continued to reward fluency, and she remained fluent.

Zeb felt the recognition settle in his body, calm and unremarkable. There was no impulse to correct or adjust. He did not wish for her to be different. He did not wish to be elsewhere.

They were coherent together. Effective. Sufficient by the room's measure. Insufficient by his.

They continued on without friction—laughing when required, listening when asked, moving through the remaining hours as if nothing had shifted at all.

Because nothing had.

And yet something had been named and left where it lay.

This was the arrangement.

Aftermath

The evening dissolved without ceremony.

Guests departed in small clusters, their goodbyes warm and unhurried. Laughter softened as people stepped toward the door, voices lowering instinctively as the house began its return to stillness. Compliments were exchanged, plans floated and loosely anchored, gratitude expressed without urgency.

Vivienne moved through these final moments with the same ease she had carried all night. She stood near the entry, accepting thanks, placing a hand briefly on an arm, offering a smile that felt both personal and complete. Nothing lingered. Nothing asked to be extended.

When the last door closed, the house began to reset.

Staff moved through the rooms quietly, collecting glasses, straightening chairs, erasing the evening with practiced discretion. Music faded and then disappeared. Lights shifted into their night register. Surfaces returned to their intended clarity.

The house reclaimed itself quickly.

Vivienne watched this process with calm satisfaction. She poured herself a glass of water and leaned lightly against the counter, scrolling through messages that had arrived during the evening. A few she answered immediately. Others she flagged for the morning.

"It went well," she said, not seeking confirmation.

Zeb nodded once. "It did."

The exchange required nothing more.

They stood together for a moment in the kitchen, the air settling around them. There was no exhaustion in her posture, no residual tension. The evening had given her exactly what she expected of it.

Zeb felt the same calm, but of a different kind.

He did not replay conversations or measure responses. He did not linger on what had been said or unsaid. The clarity he felt did not require review. It rested easily, already integrated.

They moved through the final routines side by side. Vivienne checked that a message had gone through. Zeb rinsed a glass and set it in the rack. Lights were turned off in rooms neither of them had entered.

When they reached the bedroom, Vivienne changed quickly and slipped beneath the sheet, the day already resolved for her. Zeb followed, turning off the lamp, letting the dark settle without adjustment.

She reached for him briefly, her hand resting against his arm. The contact was familiar, reassuring, unexamined. He held it there for a moment, then she let go and turned onto her side.

Her breathing slowed.

Zeb lay awake a little longer, not restless, not waiting. The quiet did not press. It did not invite thought.

Nothing in the house felt different.

Nothing had shifted outwardly. The arrangement remained intact, elegant, sufficient by every visible measure.

And yet, something had finished.

The measure had been taken—not argued, not contested, not corrected—and it did not change.

Zeb closed his eyes and let the stillness hold, knowing it now for what it was.

The house rested.

The evening was complete.

And somewhere beneath that completeness, the first irreversible knowing had settled, calm and unmoving, where it would remain.

CHAPTER 7

The Measure Between Them

The house was quiet in the way it often was before the evening settled. Not empty—prepared. Light held in place by glass. The ocean beyond reduced to movement without sound. Staff had finished their work and withdrawn without leaving evidence behind.

Vivienne sat at the long table near the windows with a tablet open in front of her. She had changed clothes already—something softer, unstructured, the kind she wore when the work of being seen was finished for the day. Her hair was loose. A glass of water rested to her right, untouched.

Zeb stood near the counter, rinsing a mug. He dried it carefully and set it upside down on the towel. He did not return it to the cabinet. He leaned his hands against the edge of the counter and stayed there.

They had been moving around each other for several minutes without speaking.

It was not tense. It was precise.

Vivienne looked up first.

"Did you want to eat in or go out?" she asked.

"Either," Zeb said.

She nodded, accepting the answer as genuine. "We could do something simple," she said. "There's no reason to make a thing of it."

"No," he agreed. "There isn't."

She glanced back down at the screen, scrolled once, then stopped. She set the tablet aside instead of closing it.

"You've been quiet," she said.

He smiled faintly. "I usually am."

"Yes," she said. "But quieter than usual."

He considered this, not to decide what to say, but to see if anything needed correcting.

"I don't feel particularly quiet," he said.

Vivienne tilted her head, studying him—not critically, not defensively. The way one studies a familiar structure to see if anything has shifted.

"Hm," she said. "Okay."

She let the moment rest, then asked, "Are you tired?"

"No."

"Bored?"

"No."

She waited. Zeb did not fill the space.

Vivienne smiled a little, not unkindly. "You know," she said, "you don't have to manage everything so carefully."

"I'm not managing," Zeb said. "I'm listening."

"To what?"

He thought about it. "To what holds."

That caught her attention. She leaned back slightly in her chair. "Enough for what?"

"For the room," he said. "For people. For me."

Vivienne considered this, her expression thoughtful rather than guarded.

"Well," she said, "I think the room usually tells us that."

Zeb nodded. "It does."

"And you think it's wrong?" she asked, not accusatory. Curious.

"No," he said. "I think it's accurate."

She smiled at that. "Accurate is good."

"It is," Zeb agreed. "It's just not the same as sufficient."

Vivienne paused.

"That sounds like philosophy," she said lightly. "Or economics. I'm never sure which."

Zeb smiled. "They overlap."

She laughed once, softly. "Everything overlaps if you look hard enough."

"Not everything," he said.

She studied him again, more carefully this time. "Say more," she said.

Zeb did not answer immediately. He did not need to search for words, but he did need to decide whether to use them.

"When you host," he said finally, "the room works. People feel held. Seen. Comfortable. You're very good at that."

"I know," Vivienne said, without vanity.

"I know you do," Zeb said. "And you should."

She waited.

"But there are other measures," he continued. "Things the room doesn't register because it doesn't need to."

"Like what?"

"Like cost," he said. "Not financial. Human."

Vivienne's expression remained open, but something in her posture shifted—attention sharpening, not closing.

"You mean labor," she said.

"Yes."

She nodded. "Of course there's labor. That's how the system functions."

"I know," Zeb said. "I'm not criticizing it."

She studied his face, searching for pressure that wasn't there.

"Then what are you doing?" she asked.

"Accounting," he said.

She smiled again, smaller this time. "You always did like balance sheets."

"They tell you what you're spending without noticing," Zeb said.

Vivienne leaned forward, elbows on the table now.

"And you think we're overspending," she said.

"No," Zeb said. "I think we're spending efficiently."

"That sounds like praise."

"It is," he said. "Efficiency is impressive."

"But," she said.

"Efficiency isn't the same as meaning," Zeb said.

Vivienne sat back.

"For you," she said.

"Yes," he said.

She considered that. "Not for me?"

Zeb did not rush to reassure her. "Not in the same way," he said.

Vivienne exhaled slowly, not irritated, not defensive. Thoughtful.

"I don't think meaning has to be heavy," she said. "Or visible. Or difficult."

"I don't either," Zeb said. "But I think it has to be carried somewhere."

"And you don't think it is," she said.

"I think it's carried beautifully," he said. "Just not by the room."

Vivienne was quiet for a moment.

"You know," she said finally, "people feel better after they leave here."

"I believe that," Zeb said.

"And that matters," she said. "It matters to me."

"It should," he said.

She looked at him steadily now. "And to you?"

He met her gaze fully. "It matters," he said. "Just not enough."

The silence that followed was not tense. It was weighted.

Vivienne broke it first.

"You've seen more than most people," she said. "Of course this feels... insufficient to you."

Zeb did not correct her.

She continued, gently now. "But not everyone needs that scale. Not everyone wants to live at that depth all the time."

"I know," he said.

"And you don't expect me to," she said.

"No," he said. "I don't expect anything."

She studied him again, searching for demand.

"Then what is this?" she asked.

Zeb considered the question carefully.

"This is me noticing," he said. "That the measure you use works perfectly. And that I'm using a different one."

Vivienne absorbed that.

"We're measuring the same life," she said slowly.

"Yes," Zeb said.

She nodded once.

"Well," she said, after a moment, "lives can hold more than one measure."

"Sometimes," Zeb said.

She smiled faintly. "You don't think this one can."

"I think it already does," he said. "Just unevenly."

Vivienne laughed softly, shaking her head. "You always do this," she said. "You make things sound so calm when they're actually… enormous."

"They're only enormous if you push them," Zeb said.

She looked at him for a long moment, then said, "You're not leaving."

It was not a question.

"No," Zeb said. "I'm not."

She nodded, relieved without showing it. "Good."

They sat there for another moment. Nothing resolved.

Vivienne reached for her water and took a sip.

"So," she said, "dinner in or out?"

Zeb smiled.

"In," he said.

"Simple?"

"Yes."

She stood and moved toward the kitchen, already thinking through options.

Zeb remained where he was for a moment longer, feeling the conversation settle into place.

Nothing had been resolved.

But the measure between them no longer hid.

CHAPTER 8

The Interval

The first week passed without distinguishing itself from the next. Zeb woke before the light finished settling into the rooms. The island moved through its early routines—maintenance carts crossing service paths, systems adjusting air and temperature with near-silent precision. He dressed, ran the shoreline, showered, walked to the clubhouse. Coffee. The paper opened, then folded again. Headlines changed. The weight of the pages did not.

When he returned, the house was already prepared.

Not active—reset. Beds made. Surfaces cleared. Whatever had occurred the day before had resolved itself into order without residue. The house did not remember.

Vivienne moved forward through her mornings with unbroken continuity. Calls returned. Messages sent. Plans confirmed. She spoke of lunches, arrivals, what would need to happen later in the week.

Her days advanced cleanly, one event giving way to the next without friction.

Zeb listened. He answered when asked. He did not interrupt the flow.

Meals repeated themselves with slight variation. Breakfast earlier one day, later the next. A different arrangement of fruit. Coffee stronger or weaker. Nothing that required notice. Evenings followed familiar arcs—dinner prepared or ordered, conversation unfolding easily, silence returning on schedule.

The weather shifted subtly. One morning cooler than the last. Another heavier with humidity. The ocean adjusted accordingly, its surface changing texture but not direction. The tide rose and fell with patient regularity.

The house absorbed each day and released it intact.

Zeb remained present inside the repetition. He attended. He assisted. He carried out the small tasks that kept things moving smoothly. His routines did not falter. If anything, they became more precise, less encumbered by thought.

The days did not ask him to do anything.

They did not demand speech or action or confrontation. They simply stayed where they had settled, altering nothing outwardly while changing the way endurance felt from the inside.

Endurance had once carried weight. Now it felt thinner—not insufficient, but no longer meaningful on its own.

Vivienne did not notice the difference.

She moved through the days as she always had, the arrangement holding. The system continued to reward fluency. Nothing resisted her.

At night, the house returned to its polished stillness. Lights dimmed. Sound softened. Glass reflected only darkness and faint interior glow. Sleep arrived easily.

Zeb lay beside her and felt the familiarity of staying without the reassurance it once provided.

Nothing had changed.

That was the change.

Absence in Motion

Vivienne left on a Tuesday morning.

Not abruptly. Not with finality. The departure unfolded the way departures always did in this house—suitcase placed by the door, shoes chosen carefully, timing adjusted by minutes rather than emotion.

She moved through the bedroom with practiced efficiency, selecting what she needed, discarding what she didn't. The room did not register the difference. Neither did she.

Zeb stood near the doorway and watched her pack. He offered to carry the bag. She nodded once, grateful but untroubled.

"I'll be back Friday next week," she said. "Unless things run late."

"Okay," he said.

She kissed his cheek—light, habitual—and took her phone from the dresser. Her attention shifted outward immediately, already elsewhere.

At the door, she paused long enough to say, "Don't forget dinner with John on Thursday. They moved it earlier."

"I won't," Zeb said.

She smiled, satisfied, and stepped out.

The house closed around her absence without resistance.

Zeb carried on with his routines. He woke early, ran the beach, showered, walked to the clubhouse. He read the paper at his usual table, folded it, left it behind. When he returned, the house was quiet but not expectant.

Messages arrived intermittently.

Landed.

Dinner went long.

Thursday moved to Friday.

Zeb replied when required. Short acknowledgments. No questions attached.

Got it.

Okay.

The exchanges ended cleanly, without residue.

The days unfolded smoothly. Staff moved through their schedules. Rooms were cleaned, reset, returned to their neutral state. Meals were prepared and cleared without ceremony.

Midweek, a message arrived from a number he associated with movement rather than invitation. A name he had not seen in months. One line of context. One question that did not assume an answer. The timing was open. The need was not.

Zeb read it once and did not respond. He placed the phone face down.

He did not need to answer to feel the shift.

Zeb ate alone some evenings, not marking the difference. He sat at the kitchen counter or outside near the glass wall, the ocean present but held at its usual distance. He did not dwell on her absence. He did not anticipate her return.

When she was away, the house did not feel emptier. It felt paused, as it often did between uses. Beauty held itself in place, intact and patient.

Vivienne's life continued seamlessly.

Her messages referenced meetings, dinners, people Zeb did not know. The tone was efficient, factual. She did not apologize for being busy. There was nothing to apologize for.

Zeb read her words without inflection and set the phone aside.

He did not miss her.

Not because he did not care—but because nothing in the rhythm had been disrupted. This was how the arrangement functioned. Her absence was one of its expected states.

The House Without Witness

With Vivienne gone, the house stretched.

Not outward, not visibly—but in duration. Hours passed without interruption. Afternoons arrived without announcement. The rhythms that once segmented the day loosened and thinned.

Zeb noticed it first in how little he needed to move.

He crossed fewer rooms. Left lights untouched. Chose the same chair twice without considering alternatives. The house offered its full range of spaces, but nothing drew him toward them.

Some rooms went unused for longer than they ever had.

One afternoon, a door down the corridor failed to close fully, stopping short of its frame. The soft click he expected never came. Air moved through the gap, subtle but persistent, carrying with it a faint exterior sound he could not place. He stood for a moment, listening, then closed the door himself.

The glass walls reflected only him and space.

At night, reflections flattened into darkness punctuated by his movement—a figure crossing, pausing, turning back. The symmetry remained uninterrupted.

The house continued to regulate itself with precision. Temperature adjusted before discomfort arrived. Light softened automatically as evening set in. The systems performed flawlessly, indifferent to whether anyone noticed.

Zeb became aware that the beauty required no response.

It did not ask to be touched or occupied. It did not change in relation to him. It remained exact regardless of use, as though its purpose had never depended on presence at all.

This was not loneliness.

Nothing pressed inward. Nothing felt missing. The house did not feel emptier—it felt complete in a way that left no room for participation.

And without realizing it yet, Zeb had stopped mistaking stillness for presence.

Selective Blindness

Zeb began to notice what staying would require.

Not immediately. The realization did not announce itself. It surfaced in small moments—when he caught himself reaching for explanations that no longer held.

An invitation forwarded by Vivienne. Assumed. Efficient. He read it once and began composing a response—something brief, explanatory, accommodating. Halfway through the sentence, he stopped. The explanation already felt like translation, and the translation felt like surrender.

He deleted the draft and set the phone down. When the screen went dark, he realized he had not felt the usual impulse to justify the silence.

There was nothing to justify.

Staying would mean continuing to translate absence into independence. Treating repetition as choice.

The blindness required was not enforced.

It was offered.

He noticed how easy it would be to accept it. To remain agreeable. To let endurance stand in for devotion, the way it always had.

And just as quietly, he noticed that he no longer could.

This was not resistance.

It was refusal.

CHAPTER 9

Gilded Silence Ends

The morning held without effort. The beach below the deck lay empty, its pale curve unbroken, the sand smoothed flat as if no one had ever needed to cross it. The water was calm in the way that only came with good weather and no audience—blue deepening toward the horizon, the surface barely disturbed, light breaking cleanly across it without shimmer or drama.

Zeb stood barefoot on the deck with a mug of coffee warming his hands. The cup was plain, heavy enough to register. He leaned against the railing and let his weight settle there, not looking out so much as allowing the view to exist without demand.

This was the hour he trusted most.

Not early enough to feel stolen. Not late enough to feel claimed.

The house behind him was quiet, sealed into its daytime stillness. No staff. No arrivals. No cues waiting to be followed. Just the soft, ambient hush of a place designed to perform even when no one was present.

He sipped the coffee and felt it register—heat first, then bitterness, then the familiar grounding that came not from pleasure but from reliability. He drank slowly, without moving, letting the world arrive at its own pace.

His mind did not race.

It widened.

Egypt surfaced first—not the heat or the noise, but the weight of standing still in crowds that carried history on their backs. Streets that never paused long enough to admire themselves. Dust in the throat. The sound of chanting folding in on itself. The unmistakable sense that things had already shifted long before anyone agreed on what to call it.

Africa followed—not as a place, but as a different measure of time. Days did not end; they layered. What mattered unfolded when conditions aligned, not when clocks insisted. Decisions arrived slowly or all at once, carried by relationships rather than schedules. Waiting there was not delay—it was participation. He remembered the look in certain eyes: people who knew exactly how much they were carrying, even when no one else noticed.

Washington arrived differently. Cleaner. Sharper. A city fluent in abstraction and consequence. Rooms where words replaced bodies, and urgency disguised distance. He had learned there how to let others exhaust themselves with motion while he watched for what did not move.

Asia came last—fragmented, layered. Airports and boardrooms. Cities that never asked to be understood, only navigated. He had learned there that efficiency could coexist with indifference, that progress did not require intimacy.

And then there were other places where darkness was given architecture. Fear had corridors and thresholds. People learned which subjects to circle and which to leave sealed. It was not belief he encountered there, but restraint—the discipline of not inviting certain forces too directly into the light.

The places did not compete.

Each had taught him something different about motion—when it mattered, when it lied, when it disguised itself as stability. None of them had offered rest. None of them had pretended to.

He took another sip of coffee and felt the warmth settle lower this time, his shoulders easing almost imperceptibly.

There were scars. Few, but real.

Not the kind that demanded recounting. Not the kind that justified anything. Marks left by decisions made cleanly and lived with fully. People he had failed by staying too long. People he had failed by leaving too early. Work misjudged. Moments where restraint had been mistaken for absence.

He did not catalogue them.

He acknowledged them.

They were part of the weight he carried without complaint.

Behind him, the house remained flawless.

Glass, light, architecture holding itself in balance. A place that asked nothing from him now that it had already delivered everything it was meant to. He did not resent it. He did not romanticize it. It had served its purpose with precision.

The coffee was nearly gone when he noticed the quiet had shifted—not deepened, not lifted, just changed register. The day had fully arrived. The beach remained empty.

Later, as the afternoon thinned into evening, he returned to the deck with a glass of bourbon.

This one he drank more slowly. Not ceremonially. Just attentively. The amber caught the last of the sun and held it briefly before dark settled in. The ocean below reflected less now, its surface flattening into a darker plane, movement suggested rather than displayed.

This was the hour where people usually mistook reflection for decision.

Zeb did not.

He let the day pass through him without shaping it into meaning. He felt the accumulated motion of years settle—not into longing, not into regret, but into something steadier. A readiness that did not require language.

He was not leaving because something had gone wrong.

He was leaving because staying would require blindness.

The bourbon burned briefly, then warmed. He finished the glass and set it down, the sound absorbed immediately by the space around him.

When he stood, it was not with resolve.

It was with alignment.

Inside, the house waited without expectation. His things were there. More than a bag's worth. A life arranged with care, ease, and surface coherence.

He would choose only what needed to move.

Not because the rest did not matter.

Because it no longer needed him.

He stepped inside, closing the door behind him with the same quiet the house had always preferred.

The ocean continued its work without witness.

And Zeb moved toward the bedroom—not to leave yet, but ready now to do so without rehearsal.

Quiet Preparation

Zeb began to prepare without marking the moment.

No pause separated before from after. He took a bag from the closet and set it on the bed—not the largest, not the smallest. One he had carried before.

He placed inside what was necessary. Clothes chosen for function. Shoes at the bottom, soles turned inward. Toiletries gathered without inventory.

Nothing symbolic entered the bag.

He did not touch the objects that anchored the house to Vivienne's world. They remained where they were.

He rinsed a mug. Wiped a counter. Closed a cabinet door left slightly ajar.

These were not gestures of farewell.

They were habits completing themselves for the last time.

Nothing resisted him.

Nothing invited him to stay.

The Step

Zeb closed the door behind him.

The sound was soft, absorbed almost immediately. The house did not register protest or loss. It remained balanced, immaculate, complete.

He stepped forward.

There was no backward look.

The house had given him exactly what it was designed to give. It had not failed him. It had simply finished.

Behind him, the glass reflected only itself now—clean lines holding an interior that no longer required witness.

Nothing collapsed.

The door had not opened on its own.

He stepped through.

Zeb walked on.

The path away from the house was unremarkable. Gravel pressed lightly beneath his shoes. Ordinary sounds somewhere ahead—distant sounds receding rather than beginning.

He felt alignment complete itself in motion.

Behind him, nothing had been destroyed.

Nothing had been corrected.

Something had been crossed.

At the end of the path, his car waited where he had left it, unremarkable, unlocked.

He did not pause.

The engine turned over without resistance. Headlights cut briefly across the glass behind him before the dark took it back.

He would not cross back.

PART II: LONGING

CHAPTER 10

Elsewhere

Zeb woke before the city did. The room was spare and unremarkable. White walls that held no intention. A narrow desk pushed against the window. Curtains that did not quite meet, leaving a thin seam of early light to mark the morning without insisting on it. The air carried unfamiliar sounds—traffic beginning to assemble itself, a voice calling from below, something metal being rolled across concrete with no concern for who might be listening.

He lay still for a moment, not to hold on to sleep, but to locate himself.

Elsewhere.

The word did not arrive as relief. It arrived as orientation.

He had not come here to rest. He had come to see what remained once the structures that shaped him were removed—once no room waited to receive him, once no one required him to be sufficient in any particular way. Elsewhere was not distance. It was a testing ground.

He stood, dressed, and stepped outside.

The street was already awake. Not in a hurry—working. Vendors setting up without ceremony. A woman sweeping dust from her doorway into a pile that would re-form by afternoon. A man drinking coffee from a chipped cup, standing rather than sitting, eyes already oriented toward the hours ahead.

Zeb walked without destination.

The movement felt different here. Less buffered. Less composed. His body adjusted without instruction, pace finding itself among other bodies moving for reasons that did not require explanation. No one watched him. No one registered his arrival. No one made room.

That, he realized, was the difference.

He passed a group of workers unloading crates from a truck parked at an awkward angle. The process was inefficient—boxes lifted twice, paths crossed and uncrossed, instructions repeated without irritation. One of the men paused to wipe sweat from his neck, glanced at Zeb, nodded once, then returned to the work without curiosity.

Recognition without extraction. Presence without interpretation.

Zeb nodded back and kept walking.

Nothing here promised improvement. The buildings were serviceable, some well kept, others simply holding. The air was heavier than he liked. The work was visible, unsoftened by design. This place did not flatter movement or elevate stillness. It did not ask to be understood.

It simply existed.

Time moved differently here.

Not faster. Not slower. It did not arrive in segments meant to resolve. It layered. Tasks overlapped without urgency, and waiting did not signal delay so much as participation. Progress appeared when conditions aligned, not when schedules demanded it. Effort accumulated quietly, without ceremony, without the illusion that it would ever be finished.

Zeb felt his attention settle downward and outward at the same time—toward hands, toward posture, toward the cost embedded in ordinary motion. He did not need to interpret what he was seeing. He did not need to translate it into meaning.

He thought briefly of the house—not with regret, not with accusation. Just as one thinks of a structure that had served its function precisely and then been left behind intact. It had not been wrong. It had simply stopped being relevant.

He did not miss Vivienne.

Not because she did not matter. Because longing had not yet found its object.

He had left places before.

Not impulsively. Not in anger.

When something was finished for him, it ended cleanly.

There were no scenes. No arguments rehearsed in advance. No lingering negotiations with what had already stopped responding. He did not circle departures, testing whether they would call him back.

He left once, without revision.

It had cost him things.

Not because leaving was wrong, but because it was complete.

He knew this about himself. He had always known it. The difference now was that he was no longer mistaking it for hardness.

He walked farther, letting the city change texture around him. Streets narrowed without announcement. Noise thickened, then thinned again. The air carried different smells—fuel, food, cigarette smoke, something chemical he could not place. He adjusted his stride without thinking, stepping around obstacles before registering them as such.

At a corner, a boy no older than twelve stood selling newspapers. Zeb bought one out of habit, folded it under his arm, did not read it. The language was unfamiliar, but the weight of the paper was not.

Later, he sat on a low wall near a construction site and watched men work in coordinated inefficiency—tasks overlapping, voices rising and falling, progress advancing by accumulation rather than plan. Nothing here was optimized. Nothing here was aestheticized.

No one was performing competence.

They were enacting it.

The work continued whether or not it was witnessed. No one paused to assess how it appeared. No one waited for acknowledgment. Effort did not disappear when unnoticed.

Zeb felt something loosen in his chest—not dramatically, not all at once. Just enough to allow his breath to deepen without effort, shoulders settling into a posture that did not brace or present.

It was not relief. But it was not nothing.

Not for a person.

For a way of being that did not require translation.

He rose and continued on.

The day unfolded without narrative. Nothing asked him to summarize the day while it was happening.

No moment leaned forward, asking to be remembered.

He noticed how rarely that occurred. No revelations announced themselves. No decisions demanded articulation. He ate when hungry. Rested when tired. Spoke when spoken to and listened when he did not. His phone stayed in his pocket until afternoon, when he checked it once, saw nothing that required response, and slipped it back without ceremony.

As evening approached, the city shifted again. Lights came on unevenly. Music drifted from somewhere above street level. People gathered briefly, dispersed, gathered again. No one marked the transitions. They happened because they happened.

Zeb found a place to eat and sat alone at a small table near the door. He ordered something simple and waited without impatience. When the food arrived, he ate slowly, paying attention to heat and texture rather than taste.

Around him, conversations rose and fell without seeking coherence.

No one asked him who he was.

No one introduced him.

He was not being placed.

For the first time in a long while, Zeb felt the absence of containment without feeling exposed. The lack of framing did not make him smaller. It simply returned scale to where it belonged.

The night settled without emphasis.

He walked back toward the room he was staying in, passing through streets that no longer required mapping. The route had already lodged itself in his body. When he reached the door, he paused—not from hesitation, but from awareness.

The day had been unremarkable.

And in that unremarkableness, something essential had occurred.

He had not been required to be sufficient.

He had simply been present.

Inside, the room was unchanged. He closed the door, set the folded paper on the desk, and sat briefly on the edge of the bed. The sounds of the city continued beyond the walls—unconcerned, ongoing, indifferent to whether he listened.

Elsewhere did not feel like arrival.

It felt like space.

Space without instruction. Space that had not yet asked him to belong.

Zeb lay down and let the noise move around him without entering. Sleep came easily, without the sensation of having reached anything, or left anything behind.

Tomorrow would not be about space. It would be about weight.

The work would begin again.

He booked the flight that night.

CHAPTER 11

The Weight of Absence

The day had already begun before Zeb arrived. There was nothing ceremonial about it. No threshold, no clear beginning. Work was already moving when he stepped into it, conversations overlapping, bodies in motion, decisions half-made and already contested.

The heat settled early and stayed.

Not the dramatic heat of postcards or warnings—just the kind that pressed into the body and refused to lift. Sweat formed without effort. Shirts clung and then dried and clung again. No one commented on it. It was simply the condition under which things happened.

Zeb stood just inside the open structure that served as the coordination point. A concrete slab, a corrugated roof, plastic chairs pulled into a loose circle that never quite held its shape. A whiteboard leaned against one wall, already marked and crossed through, dates rewritten, arrows bending back on themselves.

People moved around him without pause.

A man leaned in close to another, voices low but urgent. A woman crossed the space carrying a stack of papers pressed flat against her chest, stopping once to correct a name, then moving on before the answer arrived. Someone argued briefly near the doorway, not loudly enough to draw attention, not quietly enough to be private.

Zeb listened.

He did not interrupt. He did not gather the room. He let the disorder speak first.

This was not chaos. It was accumulation.

Meetings did not begin here. They surfaced.

Someone addressed Zeb by name, not to ask permission but to update him. A route had shifted overnight. A local organizer had not shown. Another had shown up with twice as many people as expected and no plan for how to hold them.

Zeb nodded once.

"Let's not move it yet," he said. "Let it settle."

The man hesitated—not because he disagreed, but because waiting always carried risk. Zeb saw the calculation flicker and pass.

They waited.

Outside, vehicles idled. Engines cut and restarted. Someone leaned against a truck and drank water slowly, head tilted back, eyes closed. Across the open yard, a small group practiced chants under their breath, stopping and starting, rhythm breaking and reforming without instruction.

Nothing aligned cleanly.

Nothing stopped.

Time did not move forward here.

It layered.

What had not been decided yesterday pressed into the present. What would not be decided today was already being absorbed. People waited without mistaking waiting for inactivity. Everyone carried something unfinished, and no one expected it to be resolved quickly.

Zeb moved through the space when needed.

He shifted a chair. He took a marker and rewrote a single word on the board, not correcting the plan so much as narrowing it. He answered questions without enlarging them. When someone tried to pull him into abstraction, he redirected gently.

"What happens if we don't announce it yet?" he asked once.

The question hung.

Not because it was clever, but because it acknowledged what no one wanted to say: that visibility was not always protection.

Someone nodded. Another frowned. No consensus formed. The discussion moved on.

The work was pressure.

Containment without illusion.

Zeb felt it in his body first.

The constant standing. The way shoulders lifted and never fully dropped. The small calculations repeated until they stopped feeling like thought and started feeling like posture. Hunger arrived and was ignored. Fatigue registered and was deferred.

No one sold calm.

They kept moving.

When something failed, it failed openly. When it held, it held temporarily. People adjusted without needing to be seen doing so.

Zeb did not supervise.

He wasn't there to inspire or extract, and he didn't turn effort into narrative. He didn't mistake his presence for centrality.

He was one weight among many.

A woman approached him near midday, voice tight, eyes already scanning past him.

"They're asking again," she said. "They want a statement. Something clean."

Zeb considered the heat, the bodies outside, the unfinished conversations looping back on themselves.

"Not yet," he said. "If we speak now, we lock ourselves into it."

"And if we don't?"

"We stay flexible."

She studied him for a moment, then nodded—not convinced, but willing.

She left without thanking him.

Good, he thought.

The afternoon stretched.

No resolution arrived to mark progress. Instead, small shifts accumulated. One group moved earlier than planned. Another arrived late and stayed longer. Messages came in bursts, then stopped. Phones were checked, then ignored.

Effort did not disappear when unnoticed.

Zeb stood near the edge of the space as the light shifted slightly, the heat easing just enough to be noticed. Someone handed him a bottle of water without comment. He drank half, capped it, set it down, forgot about it.

This was not the kind of work that rewarded endurance.

It consumed it.

And still, he recognized the texture—not as nostalgia, but as orientation.

This was where his attention belonged—not because it made him useful, but because it did not ask him to perform being so.

No one here cared who he had been elsewhere.

No one asked him to summarize himself.

Later, he noticed a small adjustment ripple outward.

A route that had been argued over earlier was left unannounced and moved quietly.

Two people arrived at the same conclusion without naming it.

No one traced the shift back to him.

It simply held.

He did not feel heroic.

He felt necessary in the smallest possible way.

Which was enough to keep him here.

By the time the day thinned toward evening, nothing had concluded. It never did. People began leaving in small increments, conversations trailing off without closure, plans folding back into tomorrow without being called plans.

Zeb stayed until the space emptied enough to feel different.

Not quiet.

Just less dense.

He stepped outside and let the air move across his face. The heat was still there, but it no longer pressed. Somewhere nearby, voices rose and fell, ordinary life continuing without reference to what had just been carried.

He stood there for a moment longer than required.

He wasn't reflecting or deciding—just holding the weight without converting it into meaning.

This was the present.

And it did not offer rest.

Memory Without Romance

The memory did not arrive as a story.

It came through the body first.

Zeb stood still for a moment, weight settled evenly through his feet, and felt a familiar ache surface along the backs of his hands. Not pain exactly—more like residual awareness, the way muscles remember tasks long after they have stopped performing them. His fingers flexed once, unconsciously, as if testing for grip.

He had known this sensation before.

There were jobs he had done where the day began before language. Where movement preceded thought. Where hands learned what to do faster than the mind could frame it. Lift. Carry. Hold. Wait. Adjust. Repeat.

The work had not been skilled in any way that earned recognition. It existed in transitional spaces—half-finished construction sites, temporary trailers sunk into mud, builds stalled between permits and inspections. Concrete shells where the work moved faster than the paperwork that pretended to track it.

He remembered the feel of rawness setting in before the skin broke—the warning most people ignored. Callus forming unevenly where pressure returned most reliably. Gloves helped, sometimes. Often they did not.

Meals were eaten standing.

Not by rule—by necessity. Food arrived wrapped or ladled or handed over without ceremony. No one lingered. Lingering suggested surplus—of time, of energy, of permission. None of those were assumed.

Conversation stayed practical. Who was next. What was missing. Whether the truck would arrive before dark. Jokes appeared and disappeared without needing to land.

Fatigue arrived in layers.

The visible kind—the heaviness behind the eyes, the drag in the shoulders. And the quieter kind: the fatigue of being unaccounted for.

No one was cruel about it.

Supervisors moved briskly, eyes trained on output rather than bodies. Instructions were given efficiently. Praise, when it appeared, was collective and vague. "Good work today." "We got through it."

Who exactly had gotten through it remained unspecified.

Paperwork mattered more than names. Numbers shifted on clipboards and screens. Errors were noted. Corrections implemented. People adjusted.

Zeb adjusted.

He learned quickly that visibility was not the same as presence. That being useful did not mean being seen. That silence could be misread as composure—or worse, agreement.

In these places, people learned how to occupy space without claiming it. How to rest lightly—on tailgates, curbs, unfinished steps—tools kept close, bodies arranged to minimize strain without advertising fatigue.

He watched older men measure their movements carefully before lifting, aware of backs that would not forgive miscalculation. Younger ones moved too quickly, not yet acquainted with cost.

No one framed this as hardship.

It was simply the condition.

Dignity did not come from recognition. It came from attention—from doing the task fully even when no one was watching, from not transferring frustration downward when authority remained abstract.

There were small, unspoken codes.

Sharing water without ceremony. Rotating tasks quietly so no one carried the heaviest load too long. Offering a hand without announcing it.

Respect moved laterally here, not upward.

It did not accumulate. It circulated.

And silence did different kinds of work.

There was the silence that followed a long day, when conversation fell away naturally and bodies settled into whatever rest was available. That silence held.

And there was the silence of not being addressed. Of being present only as capacity.

That silence erased.

He learned early that silence could mean rest or erasure.

The distinction mattered.

Zeb did not romanticize it.

Discomfort carried no lesson on its own.

What endured was calibration.

He learned what effort cost—lived constraint, not talking point.

Dignity did not require witness. It required attention.

Presence was earned—not through assertion or charm, but through steadiness. Through showing up where effort accumulated and not disappearing when recognition failed to follow.

The memory settled, not as longing, not as regret.

As orientation.

What Is Actually Missed

Evening arrived without announcement.

The heat loosened its grip slowly, not enough to cool the air, just enough to let the body stop bracing against it. Zeb returned to the room he was staying in and closed the door behind him. The latch caught on the second pull before settling. The walls were thin enough that the street never fully left—voices rising, a generator cycling somewhere down the block, metal striking metal and then stopping. Nothing in the room anticipated him.

He washed his hands at the small sink. The faucet required a quarter turn past what seemed sufficient before the drip stopped. He dried them on a towel that had already surrendered its softness and ate standing at the narrow counter.

The meal was simple. Rice, something stewed, bread torn rather than sliced. He did not sit because there was no reason to. The food did its work without asking to be appreciated. He ate until hunger resolved itself and stopped without ceremony.

Afterward, he leaned back against the wall and let his weight settle fully for the first time that day.

This was when the thought arrived.

Not sharply. Not as ache. Just as a shift in perception.

This would land differently if someone were here.

The sentence surprised him by its precision.

It was not I miss her. It was something else.

It was conditional. Observational.

He stayed with it, letting it finish itself without embellishment.

What would land differently was not the food. Not the room. Not the quiet.

It was the stillness.

Here, the stillness absorbed him without response. It held his body, accepted his fatigue, but returned nothing. It did not register him beyond accommodating space.

He realized then what he actually missed.

Being received without effort.

Not admired. Not evaluated. Not managed.

Just received.

He missed stillness that answered back—not with words, not with reassurance, but with presence that adjusted when he entered it. The subtle shift that occurs when two bodies share quiet and something in the air acknowledges the change.

He missed weight that moved both ways.

Not the carrying. Not the steadiness. He had carried enough for several lifetimes.

He missed the return.

The small, unremarkable resistance of another presence — neither yielding nor dominating. The sense that effort did not disappear upon contact, but met something capable of holding it.

What he did not miss clarified itself just as cleanly.

He did not miss beauty. He did not miss orchestration.

He did not miss being watched into coherence.

He did not miss the way rooms rearranged themselves around her.

He did not miss the fluency, the elegance, the ease with which everything appeared to function.

And he did not miss being managed—however gently—into sufficiency.

The absence sharpened rather than blurred.

Longing, he realized, was not emotional in the way people described it. It was directional. It pointed not toward a person, but toward a condition where presence did not have to justify itself to remain intact.

He pushed away from the wall and sat down on the edge of the bed, elbows resting loosely on his knees. His body felt heavy now, but not depleted. The kind of weight that came from having been used honestly.

What was missing was not her presence.

It was his, returning.

He lay back and let the sounds of the city continue without trying to interpret them. The room did not adjust itself around him. Nothing softened. Nothing framed the moment.

And for the first time, the absence did not feel like loss.

It felt like definition.

Something had been named—not aloud, not dramatically—but clearly enough that it would not need to be mistaken again.

Zeb closed his eyes and let the evening complete itself, knowing now what longing was doing.

Not pulling him backward.

Pointing him forward.

Encounter with Misrecognition

It happened the next evening.

Zeb had stayed later than planned at a small gathering attached loosely to the work—nothing official, nothing that required strategy. People stood with drinks in hand near open windows, the air moving just enough to keep sweat from settling. Conversation braided and unbraided without needing attention.

Someone approached him while he was listening more than speaking.

She was articulate, confident, well-informed. She knew who he was—or at least what he did. She referenced his work easily, fluently, the way people do when they have already decided where someone belongs.

"I've been following what you're doing," she said. "It's impressive. Not many people can operate at that level and still keep credibility on the ground."

Zeb nodded once. "It's a team effort."

She smiled at that, as if he had confirmed something she already liked about him.

They spoke easily after that. Too easily.

She asked questions that sounded open but arrived already shaped—about risk, about pressure, about how it felt to be in rooms where decisions were made that affected millions. She listened closely, eyes attentive, posture angled toward him.

He answered plainly.

He did not dramatize. He did not minimize. He stayed accurate.

She leaned in slightly when he spoke, as if proximity itself might extract something additional. When he paused, she filled the space quickly—not interrupting, but preventing silence from doing any work.

At one point she laughed and said, lightly, "You must get used to being the most interesting person in the room."

Zeb smiled, polite but brief.

"I don't think rooms work that way," he said.

She tilted her head. "You're very grounded," she said. "That's rare."

The comment landed where compliments usually land—on the surface.

Zeb noticed how his body responded.

Not with resistance. Not with interest.

With neutrality.

There was no pull toward her. No aversion either. He felt no temptation to be more compelling than he already was. No urge to withhold. No urge to lean in.

The ease of the interaction was the problem.

Everything flowed without friction because nothing meaningful was being exchanged. The attention was real, but it was directional—toward him as figure, not him as presence.

She was responding to coherence, not contact.

He recognized the pattern immediately.

Charisma mistaken for connection.

Intensity mistaken for depth.

Attention mistaken for reception.

None of it offended him.

None of it tempted him.

He disengaged gradually, the way one exits a room without needing to announce departure. His answers shortened. His pauses lengthened. When someone else entered the conversation, he let the shift complete itself.

"It was good talking to you," she said as he stepped back.

"It was," he agreed.

And it had been—by the measure she was using.

Zeb walked away without replaying the exchange. There was nothing to evaluate, nothing to regret. The interaction had clarified its own limits without requiring rejection.

As he stepped outside, the air felt heavier but more honest. The noise from the street moved toward him without framing or invitation. He breathed more deeply without realizing he had been holding anything back.

This, too, was useful.

The encounter confirmed what longing was not looking for.

Not admiration. Not curiosity.

Not ease mistaken for intimacy.

It wasn't chemistry.

It was the wrong measure.

Zeb continued on, unburdened by the absence of spark, untroubled by the lack of temptation. Nothing had been lost.

Something had been ruled out.

And that was necessary groundwork for what came next.

Absence Becomes Weight

Zeb returned to his room after the night had settled fully.

The building was quieter now—not hushed, not careful, just done with the day. Somewhere below, a door closed. A radio played briefly and then went silent. The city adjusted itself into evening without ceremony.

He set his bag down and did not open it.

He washed his hands at the small sink, noticing the grit that lingered even after the water ran clear. He dried them slowly and sat on the edge of the bed, letting his body register the day without asking it to explain anything.

The absence was still there.

But it no longer felt hollow.

Earlier, absence had been a lack—an open space he moved through without resistance, something neutral enough to ignore. Now it had weight. Not heaviness, not pressure. Direction.

It leaned somewhere.

He noticed the shift in his body first.

His shoulders settled lower than they had in weeks. His breathing slowed without instruction. The subtle vigilance that had once kept him upright—alert, contained, enduring—released its hold.

Endurance was no longer required.

What replaced it was something quieter and less defended.

Availability.

He understood now what he could receive. Presence without extraction.

He could receive presence that arrived without demand. That stayed when nothing needed to be managed. That returned weight rather than absorbing it.

And just as clearly, he understood what he could not return to.

He could not return to being admired instead of met. To being managed instead of held. To stillness that functioned as containment rather than contact.

That life had not been false.

It had been insufficient.

Zeb lay back and let the mattress dip slightly beneath him. The room received his weight without adjustment. The sounds outside continued without regard for his attention.

He did not reach for his phone.

He did not replay the past.

He did not imagine the future.

Longing no longer pulled him backward. It no longer searched widely.

It narrowed—cleanly, deliberately—toward what could meet him without distortion.

He was not healed.

Nothing had been repaired.

But he was no longer lonely.

The absence had done its work.

He was available.

CHAPTER 12

A Different Stillness

The place was not chosen. Zeb stopped there because the morning required pause. The street widened slightly at the corner, enough to loosen the flow of foot traffic without interrupting it. A café occupied the edge of the space, its doors already open. Tables were arranged close together—not to invite lingering, but to accommodate it when it happened anyway. The chairs did not match. Some bore scratches polished smooth by years of use. Others leaned subtly, their imbalance corrected by folded paper tucked under one leg.

The light was neutral.

Not warm. Not cold. It fell evenly across the stone pavement and through the open front, flattening surfaces rather than flattering them. Shadows existed, but they did not perform.

Inside, sound accumulated without hierarchy. Cups were set down. Cutlery shifted. A low radio played in a language Zeb did not speak, the announcer's voice steady, unhurried, threading between syllables of music he didn't recognize. Near the window, a man spoke into his phone in short bursts, his tone practical, his words clipped and local.

Zeb ordered coffee in careful phrases and stepped aside.

There was nowhere obvious to sit.

Most of the tables were already occupied—not fully, not possessively, but enough to discourage assumption. A few stools lined the interior wall. He took one, setting his bag beneath his feet, resting his forearms lightly on the narrow counter. The bar top bore old rings where cups had been lifted and replaced over years without anyone thinking to clean them away.

He waited.

A woman arrived several minutes later with her coffee and paused near the counter, scanning the room—not uncertain, just assessing. For a moment, there was no space that clearly belonged to her.

Her gaze moved past the tables, past the locals settled into familiar postures, and landed on Zeb.

She glanced at the stool beside him.

"Is anyone sitting here?" she asked, in English.

"No," he said, shifting slightly to give the chair more room.

She sat.

The exchange ended there.

She placed her cup carefully, aligning it with the edge of the counter, then reached into her bag for something he did not see.

Zeb returned his attention to the street.

Traffic moved in uneven waves—delivery carts threading between pedestrians, a bus pulling up too far from the curb, passengers stepping down anyway. A man pushed a stack of plastic crates past the café entrance, wheels rattling briefly over the stone before smoothing out again.

The city did not present itself.

It continued.

After a few minutes, the woman set a folded napkin down and asked, without turning toward him, "Do you know if the harbor ferries are running on the usual schedule today?"

"I think so," Zeb said. "They were earlier."

She nodded. "Thanks."

That was all.

She took a sip of her coffee, winced slightly at the heat, then set it back down. Zeb noticed only because the movement registered in his peripheral vision, not because it drew him in.

A breeze moved through the open front, lifting a few napkins, carrying with it the smell of coffee and something fried—oil and bread—from farther down the street. The radio crackled, then settled again into speech.

Zeb adjusted his posture, resting one foot against the rung of the stool. His body felt available, but not directed.

The woman checked her watch, then her phone, then slipped it back into her bag without typing anything. She exhaled.

Zeb mirrored the breath without noticing.

They sat in parallel silence.

It did not ask to be filled.

After a while, she turned slightly—just enough to angle her body toward him without facing him directly.

"Are you working nearby?" she asked.

"Yes," he said.

She waited.

"And you?" he asked.

"For now," she said. "It changes."

He nodded.

A server passed behind them, refilling cups without comment. Zeb moved his elbow to make space. The woman noticed and adjusted her bag with the same economy. No words were exchanged.

The city continued around them.

A dog barked briefly and was silenced. Someone laughed across the street. A horn sounded once, then stopped.

The woman stirred her coffee slowly—not because it needed stirring, but because the spoon was already there.

"Do you come here often?" she asked.

"No," he said. "Just when it's convenient."

She smiled faintly—not at him exactly, but at the answer.

"That's probably the right way," she said.

"Probably," he agreed.

Another silence settled.

They occupied it without effort.

The woman finished her coffee and stood, slinging her bag over one shoulder. She hesitated, then said, "It was nice sitting."

"Yes," Zeb said. "It was."

She nodded once and stepped back into the street, absorbed almost immediately into the flow of movement.

Zeb did not watch her go.

He remained where he was, hands resting lightly on the counter, until the moment loosened and passed.

Nothing had been claimed.

Nothing had shifted outwardly.

The morning continued.

The Dinner

The restaurant sat on the edge of the water as if it had been there before the city learned how to advertise itself.

Stone steps led down from the street to a low entrance framed in dark wood. Inside, the light was disciplined—lamps shaded, candles contained in thick glass, reflections softened rather than multiplied. Linen covered the tables without whiteness-as-performance. The glassware was heavy. The silverware carried a weight that slowed the hand.

Nothing glittered. Everything held.

Through the tall windows, the water moved with working indifference. Ferries slid past in the distance, their wake flattening behind them. A horn sounded once, far off, and the room did not react. The city outside ran on schedules that did not care what was being decided over dinner.

Zeb arrived a few minutes early.

Not from eagerness. From respect for timing—the cleanest kind of courtesy. He gave his name at the host stand and was led past a cluster of tables that carried voices low and controlled, the kind that assumed they would be heard without needing to be raised.

He noticed the staff first.

Not their faces. Their movement.

They moved like people who had learned to prevent friction before it formed. A hand appeared to adjust a glass without interrupting a sentence. A chair was shifted by inches so a coat could be hung without the wearer thinking about it. Each gesture had the economy of repetition. Nothing asked to be thanked.

His table was in the back, angled toward the windows but not offered as a view. It was positioned for privacy more than spectacle—an arrangement that implied the restaurant understood why certain people preferred not to be seen clearly.

Zeb sat, placed his phone face down, and let the room finish forming around him.

A menu was set in front of him. Thick paper, minimal ink. The kind of menu that assumed you knew what you were ordering before you opened it.

He did not open it immediately.

He watched the water move beyond the glass. The ferry lights blinked in steady intervals, indifferent to the existence of this table. That steadiness calmed something in him—not soothing, not comforting. Calibrating.

The clients arrived together.

Two men, mid-to-late fifties, tailored without flash. Their jackets were cut perfectly, but the fabric did not announce itself. Watches that did not ask to be noticed. Shoes that had never known scuffing. Their hair was carefully maintained without vanity.

They moved like men who did not have to rush because nothing required them to.

They greeted Zeb with warmth that held no risk.

"Zeb," the taller one said, extending a hand. His accent was present but not heavy. His English had the polished rhythm of boardrooms and private schools. "We are glad you could come."

His smile was practiced, not false—simply calibrated to produce agreement.

Zeb stood, shook his hand, then the other. Firm. Brief. No squeeze for dominance. No overhold for intimacy.

"Thank you," Zeb said. "I'm glad we could make it work."

They sat.

One of them—shorter, thicker through the shoulders—looked at the room as if it belonged to him, not because he owned it, but because his presence had the effect of ownership. He spoke to the waiter without turning his full attention toward him.

"Vodka," he said. "Cold. Nothing extra."

The waiter nodded as if the phrase had been spoken many times in this room.

The taller man smiled at Zeb. "You drink?"

"I drink," Zeb said.

"Good," the man replied, as if that settled something about trust.

A woman approached to pour water.

She was in her late twenties, maybe early thirties. Dark hair pinned back. Black dress, plain. Her face was striking in a way that would have drawn attention in any room, but here—under controlled light, among controlled men—beauty became just another category of object to be managed.

The shorter client's eyes tracked her with the smooth entitlement of someone who never considered the act of looking to be a request.

When she leaned in to fill his glass, he spoke to her in the local language, a phrase Zeb did not catch fully but understood in tone. The woman's mouth tightened by a fraction. She smiled anyway and moved on.

The taller man laughed softly. "You see?" he said to Zeb, in English, as if translating a joke. "Here, everyone is beautiful. It becomes... background."

Zeb looked at the woman's hands as she moved.

They were steady. Slightly dry at the knuckles. The kind of hands that washed and dried glass repeatedly. The kind that had learned to handle heavy trays without trembling, even when treated as decoration.

He met her eyes briefly when she returned to their table with a small plate of bread and a dish of oil.

"Thank you," he said.

Not warmly. Not charmingly. Simply accurately, as if the word meant what it was designed to mean.

Her expression did not change much, but something in the air became less brittle.

The menus were opened.

The taller client began performing familiarity with the offerings. He spoke as if reading were beneath him.

"This fish is excellent here," he said. "They do it properly. Not like London, where everything is a performance. Here, it is… tradition."

The shorter one snorted. "Tradition is just performance that survived."

He pointed at a line on the menu. "This. And the lamb also. And the small salads."

He did not look at Zeb, as if the table's decisions were collective by default.

Zeb scanned the menu once.

He could have mirrored their fluency. He could have asked about specials and preparations, named regions, referenced vintages. He could have done the social work of signaling he belonged in their category.

He didn't.

He didn't need to.

When the waiter returned, Zeb ordered a grilled fish and a simple side. No modifiers. No story. Just food.

The shorter client lifted an eyebrow, amused. "You eat like a soldier."

"I eat like someone who wants to be awake afterward," Zeb said.

The taller man laughed again, approving. "Practical. Very American."

"Not American," Zeb said evenly. "Not in that way anyway."

The taller man's smile held. "No?"

"No," Zeb repeated. Then, without stiffness, "But I've learned that meetings go better when your body isn't negotiating against you."

That landed.

Not as humor. As competence.

Wine arrived.

A bottle was presented with ceremony that the clients accepted as their due. The taller man began discussing the vintage with the waiter, pronouncing the name carefully, as if he enjoyed the act of being knowledgeable more than the flavor itself.

The shorter one waved a hand. "Bring it. Good. We are not poor."

The waiter nodded.

Zeb watched the bottle tilt, the red collecting in the glass. The smell rose—dark fruit, something woody. It was good wine. He knew that. He also knew he didn't want it.

When the waiter asked what Zeb would like, Zeb didn't hesitate.

"Bourbon," he said. "Neat. Whatever you have that isn't trying to prove something."

The waiter's mouth twitched, almost a smile, then he recovered. "Of course."

The taller client's eyebrows rose. "Bourbon? At a place like this?"

Zeb's answer came without defense. "At a place like this, it's useful to have something honest in your glass."

The shorter one laughed. It was the first laugh that wasn't polished. "You are... interesting," he said, as if that was both compliment and warning.

Food arrived in stages.

Small plates first. Salad arranged with restraint. Bread warm enough to be noticed. Olive oil thick, dark, peppery.

The clients ate as if the room belonged to them, which meant they ate without attention. They spoke over plates, interrupted each other, shifted the conversation without warning. Their forks were tools, not manners.

They began to talk business the way other people talked weather—casual, inevitable, as if decisions were simply a matter of moving objects from one shelf to another.

Names were dropped, but not as gossip. As proof of access.

"Of course, the deputy minister is a friend," the taller man said. "Not close. But close enough."

"Close enough is always the point," the shorter man replied.

They did not say what they wanted directly.

They didn't need to.

They spoke in the grammar of power without naming it: influence, stability, predictability, relationships. They described a situation and waited for Zeb to confirm that the situation was manageable.

Zeb listened.

Not intently. Calmly.

He asked questions only when the question produced clarity. He did not flatter. He did not feign outrage. He did not signal moral alignment.

He operated.

When they mentioned a "community initiative" with language that smelled faintly of laundering—philanthropy shaped to create leverage—Zeb didn't challenge it. He translated it into logistics.

"Who's accountable for implementation?" he asked. "And who's going to be blamed when it doesn't land the way you want?"

The taller man's eyes narrowed slightly, not in hostility. In appraisal.

"You think it will not land?" he asked.

"I think if nobody owns it, it will land wherever gravity takes it," Zeb said. "And then everyone will be surprised."

The shorter man leaned back. "You speak like you have been punished by systems."

Zeb took a sip of bourbon. The burn was familiar. It told the truth quickly.

"I've been educated by them," he said.

They liked that.

Not because it was profound. Because it suggested he would not be naive.

The waitress returned with the next course, leaning in to set plates down.

The shorter client's gaze tracked her again, slow and unhurried, like a hand reaching into a bowl without asking if it belonged to him.

He said something to her under his breath, another phrase Zeb didn't catch.

Her smile stayed in place. Her shoulders tightened.

Zeb watched her hands shift. The micro-adjustment of someone maintaining balance while being treated as imbalance.

When she set Zeb's plate down, he spoke quietly—just loud enough for her to hear.

"You can set it there," he said, making room, moving his glass, reducing the labor she had to do to accommodate him.

It wasn't gallantry.

It was the simple removal of unnecessary friction.

Her eyes met his again—brief, neutral, grateful without asking to be understood. Then she moved away.

The taller client noticed the exchange. He smiled, amused.

"You are kind," he said, as if that were an eccentricity.

Zeb didn't deny it. He didn't claim it.

He simply said, "People work."

The shorter one waved a dismissive hand. "Yes, yes. People work. But they also… enjoy attention."

Zeb did not correct him.

He didn't need to.

The dinner continued.

They ate. They drank. They spoke in confident loops, circling the same points from different angles, watching to see if Zeb would reveal himself—his hunger, his vanity, his desire to belong to their orbit.

He gave them none of it.

He gave them competence.

Nothing they could pull on later.

And as the evening stretched, Zeb felt the fatigue arrive—not from the work itself, but from the environment's assumption that extraction was normal. That everything in the room existed to be used: food, staff, conversation, bodies, time.

He stayed intact by staying simple.

When dessert was offered, the taller client looked at Zeb.

"You will have something sweet?" he asked.

Zeb shook his head. "No."

"Always disciplined," the man said, admiring.

Zeb corrected him without edge. "Not disciplined. Just finished."

The check appeared without being requested.

It was placed near the taller client, who glanced at it as if it were decorative. A card appeared. The ritual completed itself.

They stood.

There was no deal sealed. No handshakes that carried promise. No "We will do this" with certainty.

Only the sense that more conversation would follow.

Which was its own kind of hook.

The taller man clasped Zeb's shoulder with friendly pressure. "We speak tomorrow," he said, already making it true.

"Tomorrow," Zeb replied, letting it be a fact without making it devotion.

They left the restaurant together, moving up the stone steps into the night air.

The city met them with indifference.

A ferry horn sounded again, farther now. Water shifted and continued.

At the corner where they separated, the clients disappeared into a waiting car that did not idle loudly. Zeb remained on foot.

He did not watch them go.

He walked.

His body felt clean, but his nervous system carried a thin film—residue from proximity to entitlement. The kind that didn't stain, exactly, but required rinsing.

He breathed once, deep enough to reset the ribcage.

The bourbon's warmth was still in his chest, honest and uncomplicated.

He headed toward the water without deciding to.

Not as escape.

As recalibration.

Behind him, the restaurant's light remained controlled, contained in glass.

Ahead of him, the ferries moved on schedules that did not care who had paid for dinner.

The City as Equalizer

Zeb walked alone.

The restaurant's light stayed behind him, contained in glass and stone. The air outside was cooler, carrying the mixed smells of salt, fuel, and damp pavement. The night had settled without ceremony. No one marked the transition.

Along the waterfront, ferries moved on their schedules, engines low and steady. A horn sounded once, farther out—no urgency in it. Just confirmation. Water shifted against stone, absorbed the sound, continued.

Zeb followed the line of the quay without thinking about direction. His pace found itself. He did not reach for his phone. He did not rehearse the dinner or catalog what had been said. The words had already done their work and released.

Lights reflected unevenly across the water. Ripples broke them apart, reassembled them, broke them again. Nothing held long enough to become display.

People passed him without registering. A couple walked ahead, close but not touching. A man leaned against a railing, smoking, eyes unfocused. Someone laughed behind him and then didn't. The city moved at a volume that required no adjustment.

Here, hierarchy flattened.

No one could tell who had paid for dinner. No one could tell who had influence or leverage or access to rooms like the one he'd left. Jackets and watches and voices lost their relevance once unobserved.

Zeb felt the residue thin.

Not relief. Not release.

Scale.

He crossed a street where the pavement narrowed, then widened again. The route folded back toward itself without announcement. The sounds shifted—less water now, more footsteps, the low hum of traffic threading through side streets.

The café appeared without signaling.

Same open front. Same uneven chairs. Same spill of light onto stone. The radio inside played something else now, or maybe the same thing at a different point. It did not matter.

Zeb slowed.

Not to stop.

Not to decide.

He stood there for a moment anyway, the city moving around him, unchanged by his presence, uninterested in what he carried.

Then the moment loosened.

And he moved on.

Quiet Echo

The café was open when Zeb passed again the following afternoon.

Not the same hour. Not the same light. The street carried more weight now—voices louder, footsteps less tentative. The morning's looseness had tightened into something functional.

He did not plan to stop.

He did anyway.

The tables were arranged as before. The chairs still mismatched, their small corrections—paper folded under a leg, a slight tilt accounted for—unchanged. The counter along the wall held its narrow stools. One was empty.

Zeb took it.

He ordered coffee without looking at the menu. The server nodded, already moving. No recognition passed between them. None was required.

The woman was not there.

He registered that without disappointment. Without relief.

Just placement.

The space felt different—not altered, but clarified. The stillness he had encountered here before did not arrive as pause this time. It did not open itself or make room for him.

It simply held.

Zeb noticed how easily his body settled into it. No adjustment. No guarding. No expectation that something should occur to justify remaining.

Around him, the café continued to function.

A couple argued quietly over something procedural. A delivery box was dragged across the threshold and lifted without comment. Cups touched saucers and separated again. The radio played beneath it all, never quite foreground.

Zeb did not scan for her.

He did not check the street to see if someone might arrive.

He drank his coffee while it was hot, then slower as it cooled. He did not time the interval. He did not assign it duration.

What registered was not absence.

It was alignment.

The stillness here no longer felt like shelter. It did not soften edges or buffer him from anything that came before. It held him at scale—neither enlarged nor reduced.

The dinner from the night before did not intrude. Its residue had already thinned to transparency. What remained was not contrast, but measurement.

This was what unextracted space felt like.

Not quiet as relief.

Quiet as reference.

Zeb finished the coffee and set the cup down where the counter had already made room for it. He stood without marking the end of the moment.

Outside, the street continued without pause.

He stepped back into it, posture unchanged, attention intact—carrying with him not an encounter, not a memory, but a standard that required no protection.

The café did not recede.

It did not advance.

It remained where it was.

It did not belong to this place.

That was the difference.

The stillness had followed him.

Continuation Without Residue

Work resumed without announcement.

The next morning, Zeb was back in the hotel room where he usually worked when he traveled alone. The desk was small and positioned badly for comfort, but it held what it needed to hold. The chair faced the window at a slight angle. He adjusted it once and left it there.

Emails required response. Documents required review. Timelines adjusted themselves as soon as they were touched. Names appeared, disappeared. Questions arrived already shaped by assumptions he did not share but understood.

He answered what needed answering.

He declined what did not.

Nothing from the dinner complicated the work. No residue bled into tone or posture. He did not carry the clients with him as reference points, nor did he resist them in absence. They remained where they belonged—in context, not in him.

A call ran long and then ended. Another was rescheduled without friction. A logistical problem surfaced and resolved itself once someone named it correctly. The day accumulated in manageable layers.

Zeb noticed that his attention remained steady.

Not sharpened.

Not dulled.

The stillness from the café did not soften his edge or slow his responses. It did not become something he reached for when the work thickened. It stayed where it belonged—as orientation, not refuge.

At lunch, he ate without ceremony, seated on the edge of the bed with the tray balanced carefully. Food, water, movement. The body accounted for itself without instruction.

Later, during a call, he stood near the window while a colleague spoke, watching the city rearrange itself below—cars pausing, then moving, pedestrians negotiating space without acknowledgment. The pattern held. It did not require supervision.

When the workday thinned, Zeb closed his laptop and left it on the desk without checking whether anything remained undone. What could be done had been done. What could not would wait.

Outside, the light had shifted again. The water moved as it had earlier, unremarked. Ferries arrived and departed on schedules that did not require his participation.

Zeb left the room and joined the street, letting it take his pace.

Nothing had displaced him.

The day continued.

CHAPTER 13

Learning the Shape of Quiet

The door opened without announcement. A shift in air. The hinge, then the room settling again. She stepped inside and paused just long enough for the room to settle around her. Not searching or scanning—just letting the space clarify.

She moved toward the stools.

The space beside Zeb remained open.

She stopped there.

"Is this taken?" she asked.

Her English was clean. Not accented in a way that asked to be decoded. Not local either.

"No."

He shifted an inch—neither inviting nor withdrawing. Just widening the margin so the stool could hold her without friction.

She sat. Rested her forearms lightly on the counter.

No surprise passed between them. No acknowledgment of repetition. Just placement.

Outside, traffic folded in on itself and released. A delivery cart rattled over stone and smoothed once it reached pavement. The radio inside shifted to a new song without anyone noticing.

"You found it convenient again," she said.

Not a question.

"Yes."

A small pause.

"You're not from here," she added.

Neither accusation nor curiosity. Just calibration.

"No."

"American?"

"Most of the time," he said.

That earned the faintest curve at the corner of her mouth.

"Tourists don't usually sit like that," she said.

"Like what?"

"As if they're not waiting for anything."

He let that settle before answering.

"I'm not."

She nodded once, accepting the correction.

The server placed a cup in front of her without asking. She touched it briefly, gauging heat.

"You work?" she asked.

"Yes."

"Nearby?"

"For now."

That seemed to satisfy her.

Silence returned, but it carried less provisional weight than before. The air did not require management. No one filled it to prevent misreading.

She lifted the cup and drank without flinching.

"You're different," she said, not looking at him.

"How?"

"Less braced."

He did not respond immediately. He noticed instead that she had said it without demand — not probing, not testing.

"Maybe," he said.

A cyclist cut too close to a taxi outside. A horn snapped once and dissolved.

"You're not local either," he said.

"No."

"But you're not visiting."

"No."

He nodded. That was enough.

She finished half the cup and stood.

"It was good," she said.

"Yes."

Not talking. Not meeting.

Just good.

She stepped back into the street without looking behind her.

Zeb did not watch her go.

He stayed long enough to confirm nothing in him was reaching.

Then he finished his coffee and stood.

The room did not change.

The city did not register the exchange.

But something had shifted shape without announcing itself.

Parallel Time

The morning did not close. It lengthened.

The room changed shape as the morning progressed.

Not abruptly—just by accumulation. Chairs filled and emptied. Cups were replaced. The radio gave way to something quieter and then to nothing at all. The café absorbed the day without announcing transitions.

Zeb had taken a table near the back wall, narrow enough that it discouraged conversation without preventing it. He set his bag beneath the chair, opened his laptop, and arranged a few papers beside it—not for display, just to keep them from folding into one another.

Across the room, the woman occupied a table of similar size.

Not opposite him. Not adjacent. Near enough that movement registered without demanding attention. Far enough that nothing about their positions implied intent.

She had a notebook open. A pen rested across the page rather than in her hand. Her phone lay face down to one side.

Zeb worked.

Emails first. Short ones. Clarifications. A line removed here, a sentence tightened there. He read more than he wrote. Paused between messages without filling the space with distraction.

Shared space usually pulled a quiet vigilance—calibration, signaling, a sense of being watched into etiquette. Here, it didn't engage. He worked the way he worked when no one was being managed.

He shifted in his chair, not to see her better, but to settle his weight. The posture held.

At some point, she stood and moved toward the counter. Zeb registered the motion only because it altered the room's balance for a moment. When she returned, she did not resume her seat immediately. She adjusted the table slightly—an inch, maybe two—to clear space for her notebook, then sat.

Zeb did not look up.

The café continued to function.

A pair of tourists attempted to decode the menu at the counter, pointing, whispering, mispronouncing. A server answered with patience that had long ago stopped requiring effort. Someone at the front took a call and spoke too loudly for the space, then corrected themselves when they noticed the room's texture.

Zeb finished one task and let the next arrive without urgency.

He realized he was not measuring time.

Not in the way he usually did—not by minutes or deadlines, but by internal thresholds. When to move. When to disengage. When to justify staying. None of those markers surfaced.

The woman wrote for a while, stopped, reread what she had written, crossed out a single line, and left the rest intact. She closed the notebook, opened it again a few minutes later, and added something in the margin.

Zeb noticed without attaching meaning.

He read a document twice, not because it was unclear, but because the second reading revealed what the first had skimmed past. When he reached the end, he did not immediately scroll back to the beginning. He let the page sit.

At another table, two men leaned close together and spoke in low voices, their heads nearly touching. Their conversation carried the faint hum of negotiation—numbers, concessions, something deferred. Zeb caught none of the details and did not try.

The woman shifted her chair back an inch and crossed one leg over the other. The movement was practical, not expressive. She rested her forearms on the table and returned to her notebook.

Zeb realized something had changed.

He was no longer checking for a signal that quiet was permissible.

In the past, silence had often functioned as a test—an interval to be passed or failed. Someone would eventually need to rescue it, animate it, turn it into something legible. Here, nothing required rescue.

The room did not thin when no one spoke.

It thickened.

People continued to enter. Others left. The space accommodated all of it without rearranging itself around any particular presence.

Zeb took a call.

He stepped just outside the café, phone to his ear, voice low. The call was brief. Logistics. A timeline confirmed. A problem reduced to sequence rather than urgency.

When he returned, he did not check whether she had noticed his absence.

She was still there.

He sat and resumed work.

At some point, she gathered her things and stood. Zeb noticed only when the chair moved. She adjusted the strap of her bag, paused as if deciding whether to leave something behind, then didn't.

"I'm heading out," she said—not to him specifically, but to the space between them.

Zeb looked up. "Okay," he said.

That was all.

She moved toward the door. Someone else stepped in to occupy the space she had vacated before the chair was fully settled back into place.

The room did not mark her departure.

Zeb returned to his screen.

He finished what he had been doing and then sat without immediately replacing it. He stayed a little longer than he would have before, not as a decision, just as the next unforced thing.

Eventually, he closed his laptop and slid it back into his bag. He did not leave right away. He drank the last of his coffee, now lukewarm, without reacting to the temperature.

When he stood, it was because standing was the next thing to do.

The room continued.

Outside, the street held its pace. Traffic shifted. A delivery truck stalled, then moved on. Zeb stepped into the flow without carrying anything with him that required explanation.

Nothing announced itself. Something settled.

Shared Meal Without Ritual

Two days later, the café held the same shape.
The table near the back wall was open again.

The table was narrow enough that two people could share it without claiming each other.

He had taken one side. She had taken the other.

There had been no agreement to sit together. It was simply the only table left in the back.

When the food arrived, it arrived to the table—not to them.

The plates were set down without ceremony. No one asked who had ordered what. The server placed them where space allowed and moved on.

Zeb adjusted his chair slightly, not to make room, just to align it with the table's edge. The woman did the same a moment later, independently, her movement registering only because it matched the table's geometry. The food steamed briefly and then settled. Whatever it was meant to smell like dispersed quickly into the ambient mix of coffee, oil, and the city pressing in through the open door.

Zeb picked up his fork and began eating.

He did not wait.

The first bite registered as food—warm, filling, unremarkable. He chewed without monitoring pace, without checking whether she had started yet. Across from him, she ate as well, neither faster nor slower, simply according to her own rhythm. Their movements overlapped without synchronizing.

Outside, something metal scraped along the pavement and was pulled away again. Inside, a chair tipped and corrected itself. Someone laughed too loudly and then lowered their voice. None of it interrupted the act of eating.

Zeb noticed that he was not paying attention to her plate.

He was accustomed to tracking shared meals as small negotiations—when to pause, when to offer, when to mirror. Here, none of that engaged. He ate when he wanted to eat. He drank water when he needed to.

They did not speak.

Not pointedly. Not as restraint. The absence of conversation existed alongside the meal the way background sound existed alongside everything else—present, unremarkable, uninterested in meaning.

The woman wiped her fingers on a napkin and folded it once, just enough to clear space. Zeb noticed without attaching significance. He continued eating.

The food did not invite appreciation. It did its job.

When he finished, he placed his fork beside the plate and leaned back slightly—not to disengage, just to change posture. There was no shared sense of completion. She took another bite. Zeb drank water.

A phone buzzed somewhere behind them and was silenced immediately.

Zeb realized then that he was not holding anything in reserve.

He was not spacing out his eating to match hers. He was not anticipating a moment where the meal would need to be named—finished, enjoyed, acknowledged.

He ate fully.

Across from him, the woman did the same. She did not comment on the food. She did not ask if he wanted more, or less, or anything else.

At some point, she stood to refill her water. Zeb remained seated. When she returned, she did not offer to refill his. He did not ask. The glass at his place was still half full.

The room continued to function.

When she finished, she set her fork down without signaling and reached for her cup.

Afterward, nothing replaced the meal.

The quiet that followed did not swell or announce itself. It simply occupied the space the food had vacated.

The woman slid her plate inward to clear space. Zeb mirrored the movement unconsciously. The table adjusted and held.

Outside, a delivery truck idled and then moved on. Inside, the radio changed tracks without comment.

After a while, she stood and returned her plate to the counter. Zeb did the same a moment later. They did not coordinate. The order did not matter.

"I've got to get moving," she said.

Zeb nodded. "I've got a call soon."

No timelines were negotiated.

They sat for another moment, the table cleared now, the space between them empty but not charged. The quiet remained intact.

The woman slung her bag over her shoulder and stepped away. Zeb remained seated, not because she had left, but because there was no reason to move yet.

She paused briefly near the door, then continued on without looking back.

Zeb stayed where he was for another minute, hands resting loosely on the table, attention unhooked. The room continued to hold itself.

When he finally stood, it was not to mark the end of anything.

It was simply time to go.

The quiet followed him as far as the street allowed.

It did not need to go farther.

Walking Without Agenda

On a different afternoon, they left at the same time and the street took them. The café door swung shut behind, sealing in its layered noise—cups, radio, the low friction of bodies adjusting. Outside: salt, exhaust, engines idling out on the water. Zeb walked with his hands empty.

He hadn't brought anything out with him except his keys and whatever remained of the day's heat in his body. The woman adjusted the strap of her bag once and let her arm fall back to her side. They took the nearest direction that required no decision: down the street that followed the slope toward the water.

There was no pace negotiation. No glance to check distance. No subtle shortening of stride. Zeb did not do what he usually did in shared movement—compute speed, allow for another rhythm, decide whether he was supposed to take the lead. He walked as he walked. Beside him, she moved with a cadence that was neither hurried nor careful. Their steps aligned and misaligned without consequence.

The city met them as it was. A narrow lane spilled them into a wider one. Motorbikes threaded through gaps in foot traffic without apology. Two men carried a long plank between them, calling out once to clear a path, not looking at anyone in particular. A woman pushed a cart of bread with one hand and spoke into her phone with the other, her voice sharp and quick, her eyes fixed forward.

Zeb registered the economy of it—how bodies solved space without translating it into meaning.

They crossed at a point that was not marked as a crossing. Cars slowed because cars were used to slowing there. Zeb stepped through a gap and felt the woman step through a different gap half a beat later. Neither of them looked back to confirm the other had made it. The assumption was not intimacy. It was ordinary competence.

A few minutes passed before either of them spoke. The woman said something about the street ahead—whether it stayed open or narrowed. It wasn't framed as conversation. It was a practical utterance, spoken at the volume of weather.

"I think it tightens up," Zeb said.

She nodded, and they kept moving.

The exchange ended cleanly. It didn't open anything that needed to be carried forward. It was just information placed down and left behind.

They turned toward the waterfront. Not to arrive there, not to make an outing of it—simply because the street curved and the flow of people carried that way. The water appeared between buildings in intermittent flashes: a sheet of gray-blue, chopped by wind, ferries dragging white wake behind them without ceremony. Stone steps descended into the edge of the quay, worn smooth by years of feet and salt.

Zeb felt the way his attention behaved in motion. Walking had always been his domain. It was where he could outlast, outpace, decide. It was where he could leave without needing to declare departure. In other cities, with other people, he would have already been scanning for the cleanest moment to diverge: an intersection, a doorway, a reason that could be spoken without being questioned.

Here, he did not search for that. He did not hold himself ready to peel away.

That absence did not feel like surrender. It felt like the absence of a requirement.

They moved along the water for a stretch. Vendors stood near the railing with trays of small things—tea, roasted nuts, paper cups stacked inside one another. A man leaned on a bollard and smoked, watching the ferries without expression. Engines moved through low cycles: idle, surge, pull away. Ropes tightened, slackened, snapped free. Metal struck dock once, clean and dull, then stopped.

The city did not make room for proximity. It made room only for movement.

They paused briefly—not together, not as a decision—at the edge of a narrow set of steps where a cluster of tourists had slowed to take pictures of the water as if it were newly invented. Zeb waited because the path required waiting. The woman shifted her weight onto one foot and looked down the line of people as if estimating how long it would take.

When the opening came, they moved again.

A few minutes later, she said something else—about the wind, or how the air changed when it passed between buildings. Zeb answered once, then let the line end. The conversation appeared, served its purpose, and dissolved without any effort spent keeping it alive.

Zeb noticed something specific: he was not shaping his quiet.

In other settings, silence in motion became something to manage—either filled to signal ease, or held to signal depth. Here, the quiet did neither. It remained what was left when nothing needed exchanging.

They walked past a storefront where a radio played too loud, a song broken by static. A man dragged a hose across the pavement, water spilling in a thin stream that ran toward a gutter already clogged with leaves. Zeb stepped over it. The woman stepped around it. Their choices did not match. The mismatch required nothing.

At a corner, the street steepened. The flow of pedestrians tightened. Someone brushed Zeb's shoulder without apologizing. A delivery cart rattled past too close, the driver's eyes fixed forward. Zeb adjusted his path by inches—not to make room for her, not to guard her—simply to keep moving.

Then the divergence happened.

The woman slowed—not abruptly, not as signal—just enough to look into a shop window where glass jars held spices in stacked color: deep red, dull gold, the brown of dried leaves. Her pace shifted by half a step, then another.

Zeb did not slow in anticipation.

He took two more strides before registering the distance opening. His body did what it had always done: prepared to keep going. To let separation become natural. To treat mismatch as exit.

He stopped. Not dramatically. Not as decision. He paused because his feet reached a point where stopping made sense—a break in the crowd, a place where he wouldn't block anyone. He shifted his weight back onto his heels and waited without reaching for his phone, without scanning for a reason that would justify the pause.

The woman finished looking. She did not call to him. She did not gesture. She simply resumed walking.

The distance between them closed as she moved forward again. Zeb started when she came back into alignment—not because she had caught up, not because he was allowing her to—because that was the next motion available. They continued without comment.

No repair language arrived. The moment stayed small. In other years he would have turned divergence into proof—freedom, or failure. Here it remained what it was: difference without narrative.

They walked another block.

A ferry horn sounded again, closer this time. The water flashed between two buildings and then disappeared. A group of children ran past, shouting in a language Zeb didn't follow, their laughter sharp and short. A man called after them once—not angry, just loud enough to be heard.

The woman adjusted her bag again and glanced up the street as if orienting herself.

Zeb saw the junction before they reached it: one street climbing inland into tighter alleys and stacked buildings, the other continuing along the water where the air stayed open and the traffic thinned.

Neither of them slowed. No mutual hesitation. No softening of pace to create a moment.

At the split, she angled inland.
Zeb felt the shift before he saw it.

For a fraction of a second, their eyes met—
not as question, not as invitation. Just recognition of direction.

Then she turned.

He continued toward the water.

There was no marking of it. No "See you." No exchange of plans. No gesture that turned separation into meaning. The city took each direction and carried it forward without distinction.

Zeb walked on with his cadence unchanged.

His hands remained empty.

The space beside him did not register as absence or loss. It registered as space—ordinary, intact, unclaimed.

He crossed another street without needing to look back.

Duration Without Yield

Time began to pass without being counted.

Not in days or dates, not in frequency or measure, but in small overlaps that did not announce themselves as pattern. Zeb noticed it first as an absence of friction. The calendar did not resist. The hours did not require explanation.

Sometimes they crossed paths in the café. Sometimes they didn't. Sometimes they sat at neighboring tables without speaking. Other times they exchanged a few words. Nothing accumulated beyond the moment in which it occurred.

The city held the rest.

Zeb worked. Meetings ran long or ended early. Calls stacked and unstacked themselves. He took notes, revised plans, responded when response was required. The rhythm of the days retained its structure. Nothing bent to accommodate anything else.

When he arrived at the café and she was already there, he sat. When she arrived later, she took a seat without comment. When one of them left first, it happened mid-thought, mid-sentence, mid-task.

No apology followed. No explanation attached itself to departure.

He noticed that his body no longer prepared for the end of encounters.

This, too, was new.

Before, presence carried a hidden timer. Stay too long and expectation formed. Leave too early and justification followed. Shared intervals accumulated cost. Something would surface later—quietly—as obligation.

Here, nothing returned demanding payment.

He did not feel lighter. He did not feel anchored. He simply remained where he was, doing what he had come to do.

Some days they walked a few blocks together after leaving the café. Other days they parted at the door. The difference did not register as choice. It registered as circumstance.

Once, she slowed near a crossing to retie a loose shoe. Zeb paused without thinking, then continued when she did. Neither of them remarked on it. The movement adjusted and held.

Another day, he turned down a side street to take a call. When he returned, she was gone. He did not look for her.

His attention did not chase continuity.

This was not discipline. It was the absence of necessity.

The city continued to make itself available without invitation. Ferries arrived and departed. The waterfront shifted color as the light changed. Workers moved through the same routes at the same hours. Dogs were walked, buses idled, crates were lifted and set down again.

Zeb found himself staying later than he had planned more than once—not to wait, not to linger, but because no internal signal told him to leave.

When he did go, it was clean.

No residue followed.

He realized that effort was no longer being stored.

In the past, even neutral interactions required accounting. A mental ledger tracked who had given, who had withheld, what had been left unsaid and might resurface later. Presence accumulated interest. Silence carried deferred charge.

Here, the ledger remained blank.

He did not feel generous. He did not feel guarded. He felt accurate.

One afternoon he noticed she had not been there all day. The realization arrived late, without spike. He registered it the way one notices a café has changed its bread or a street has been repaved—information without charge.

He worked anyway.

Another evening, he arrived to find her already seated, reading. He took a table across the room. They did not speak. When he left, she did not look up.

Nothing tightened.

Over several days, the same gestures repeated without rehearsing themselves. Coffee ordered. Chairs adjusted. Bags set down and picked up again. Plates returned. Doors opened and closed.

None of it became symbolic.

He noticed he had stopped wondering what would happen if this continued.

The question did not arise.

He had been trained, over years, to expect duration to demand resolution—that time spent together would eventually require naming: definition, escalation, withdrawal. Here, time passed and asked nothing.

That absence did not feel like avoidance.

It felt like trust without narrative.

He recognized the shift only because of what did not happen.

He did not begin preparing an exit. He did not translate presence into meaning. The familiar edge of anticipation never surfaced.

Nothing was being promised.

Nothing was being withheld.

One morning, he left the café alone and walked several blocks before realizing he had not checked his phone since arriving. The device remained silent in his pocket. He did not reach for it.

At a corner, he paused to let a group of workers pass, their conversation clipped and efficient. He watched them disappear down a side street and continued on without adjusting his pace.

Later that day, he completed a task that had been stalled for weeks. The solution arrived without effort—not through insight, but because no internal noise competed with it.

That night, he ate alone at a small place near the water. He ordered simply. The meal ended. He left.

No comparison surfaced.

He began to understand something—not as thought, but as calibration.

Presence did not require defense. It did not require vigilance. It did not require him to disappear preemptively to preserve autonomy.

It could exist, repeat, and dissolve again without claiming him.

The realization did not feel like relief.

It felt like confirmation of something his body had already accepted.

On the final day of the week, he arrived at the café and found no familiar faces. He took a seat anyway. He worked. He drank his coffee. The chair across from him remained empty.

The absence did not echo.

When he stood to leave, he did not mark the moment. He stepped into the street and merged with the movement around him.

That evening, he returned to his room, set his bag down, and reviewed his notes for the next day. The city moved outside the window, unconcerned.

He sat for a moment longer than necessary. Then he turned off the light.

Nothing had been taken. Nothing had been added.

For the first time, duration itself no longer felt adversarial.

It simply passed.

And he remained intact.

The Shape of Quiet

The café was not full, but it was never empty.

It held its own weather—cups moving, chairs shifting, the low friction of people adjusting themselves into the day. The radio played something thin and unfamiliar. A door opened and closed. A current of street air passed through and left again without altering the room.

Zeb took a stool at the counter—the same place he had taken before without ever choosing it. His bag went beneath his feet. He ordered coffee. The barista nodded, the exchange remaining exactly what it was.

He set a file on the counter and opened it.

Numbers. Notes. A timeline that would need to hold under pressure. Names written in shorthand only he would recognize. The work was ordinary. It asked for attention, not emotion.

He began.

At a table near the wall, the woman was there.

Not arriving. Not positioned. Simply present. Shoulders loose. One hand near a cup, the other resting against a page turned halfway. If she noticed him, she left it unannounced. If she did not, the effect was the same.

Zeb's posture did not change.

His attention stayed on the page in front of him. He corrected a figure. Rewrote a line. Drew a thin box around a number that would require verification. The pen moved. The work held.

A chair scraped behind him and was corrected. Someone laughed once and stopped. A server passed with a tray, balanced with the ease of repetition.

Zeb paused to reread a paragraph, then continued.

His breathing remained even.

In other rooms, quiet required management. It signaled potential—invitation, performance, obligation. Attention converted into currency. Silence became something to pass or prove.

Here, it remained what it was.

The woman stood at some point and returned her cup to the counter. He registered the motion without following it. She returned, sat again, opened her page where she had left it.

No acknowledgement passed between them.

The absence was not cold.

It was clean.

He wrote for another twenty minutes, then stretched his fingers. The ache in the joints was mild, ordinary. He pressed his thumb into the base of his palm once, then let his hand rest again.

The coffee cooled. He drank it anyway.

Across the room, she closed her notebook and placed it in her bag. She checked her phone once—not urgently—then returned it to her pocket. She remained seated.

Zeb underlined a phrase that had bothered him for two days and still did. He noted it in the margin and left it unresolved. Some things did not improve under force.

Through the open front, the street sloped toward the water. A delivery cart rattled past. A bus stopped too far from the curb and passengers stepped down anyway. A dog pulled its handler forward and was corrected without anger.

Nothing was arranged for observation.

It functioned.

Zeb felt that register in himself—not as comfort, not as relief. As proportion. The world continuing without asking him to anchor it.

He returned to the page.

A server refilled a cup beside him without asking. Zeb moved his elbow a few centimeters to make space. The server moved on. No thanks were exchanged. Nothing required softening into etiquette.

The room absorbed new arrivals. A group entered speaking too loudly; their volume settled as they sat. A table wobbled; someone folded paper beneath one leg. The radio crackled, then steadied.

Zeb finished the page and closed the file.

Not completed—just sufficient.

He sat for a moment with his hands resting lightly on the counter, gaze unfixed. The quiet did not expand into meaning. It remained structural—supportive, uninsisting.

Across the room, the woman stood, slung her bag over one shoulder, and moved toward the door. She paused long enough to leave a coin on the counter, then stepped into the street.

Zeb did not track her departure.

Nothing dipped. Nothing lifted.

The room remained itself.

He sat another minute.

Then he pulled his bag from beneath his feet and stood. The stool scraped lightly; he nudged it back into place with the heel of his shoe.

At the counter, he left some change without checking for acknowledgment.

Outside, the air carried salt and exhaust in equal measure. He walked three blocks toward the water and stopped at a crossing while traffic moved through.

A wake unstitched itself against the seawall—distant, indifferent.

When the light changed, he crossed.

On the far side, he adjusted the strap of his bag and continued without hurry.

Nothing had been proven. Nothing had been initiated.

The day moved forward.

Later, in his room, he washed his hands and set the towel back on the rack with the same precision he used elsewhere. He opened his laptop and answered the first email in the queue—two sentences, clear and sufficient.

He hit send.

Then he closed the laptop and sat on the edge of the bed, listening to the city through the window.

The quiet did not require interpretation.

It existed.

After a moment, he stood, switched off the light, and lay down.

His phone remained on the table.

Sleep arrived without negotiation—no scanning, no internal rehearsal, no background inventory of what might be missing.

In the dark, the absence that once would have hollowed him did not.

It held.

CHAPTER 14

When Devotion Costs

Nothing ended. That was the first thing Zeb noticed—not as a relief, not as disappointment, but as a condition that had quietly taken hold.

The days continued to layer the way they had been. Mornings at the café when it aligned with his schedule. Other mornings elsewhere, then back again without pattern announcing itself. Walking intervals that began and ended without coordination. Workdays that overlapped just enough to register without needing explanation. Sometimes they spoke. Sometimes they didn't. The difference no longer felt diagnostic.

No one named anything.

There was no language of "still," or "again," or "lately." No gestures that turned repetition into reassurance. Nothing was framed

as ongoing, provisional, or meaningful. The continuity did not ask to
be interpreted.

The woman remained present in the same way the city
remained present—sometimes close, sometimes not, never calling
attention to the fact of her persistence. When she was there, she was
there. When she wasn't, nothing closed around the absence.

She had never positioned herself as significant. That, too, he
registered.

He could not have described her as beautiful without feeling
imprecise. But he noticed how the room adjusted around her—how a
glance lingered half a second longer than necessary, how a server's
tone shifted by a shade when addressing her, how she absorbed it
without performing awareness. She did not capitalize on attention.
She let it pass through her as if it were ambient.

Once or twice, in moments that did not declare themselves
important, he felt the small correction in his own attention—the way
it sharpened when she lifted her cup, the tendon at her wrist
tightening briefly beneath the skin, the way her voice settled into a
register that did not reach for approval. It was involuntary. Bodily.
Information, not intention.

It passed.

It still counted.

And once—mid-afternoon, in the middle of a day he could not
later reconstruct—the thought crossed him cleanly, without
emotional lead-in:

What if I stayed long enough to learn her name?

The thought did not carry romance. It carried structure. The
recognition of an unopened door in a place he'd already been moving
through.

He did not follow it.

But it remained—not as desire, not as plan, but as possibility.

Zeb noticed that he had stopped marking beginnings.

In other places, with other people, he had always tracked the arc—first meeting, second encounter, the point where coincidence gave way to intention. He had been trained to sense when something crossed from incidental into relational, when duration required acknowledgment.

Here, nothing crossed.

The familiarity did not bloom. It thickened.

He felt it most clearly in motion—or rather, in the way motion had stopped doing what it used to do.

Walking no longer reset him.

For most of his life, movement had been his solvent. Travel dissolved residue. New locations cleared emotional buildup. Even short departures—an errand, a walk, a flight booked but not yet taken—restored equilibrium. Motion preserved autonomy by keeping him uncontained.

Now, movement still occurred, but it no longer delivered that clean release.

He walked the same routes and arrived unchanged. He traveled for work and returned without the sense of having exited anything. Even when the woman was absent for a day or two, the continuity held—not as longing, not as pull, but as default.

Staying had become the baseline.

That realization did not comfort him.

It destabilized him.

Defaults were dangerous. Defaults erased choice by making it unnecessary. He had always trusted motion because it reasserted agency without requiring explanation. Now, staying required no explanation either—and that symmetry unsettled him.

The city continued to provide exits.

Airports functioned. Trains ran. Routes remained open. He could leave cleanly, without confrontation, without consequence. The woman had not anchored him. She had not asked for anything. She had not rearranged her life to accommodate him.

And yet, when he scanned forward—only briefly, only to check—he saw fewer obvious departure points.

Not fewer exits.

Fewer reasons.

The days did not resist him. They absorbed him.

The work adjusted accordingly.

Meetings were scheduled with more flexibility. Calls shifted to accommodate time zones that would have once dictated his movement. Remote solutions replaced on-site presence. None of it felt forced. No one complained. No urgency surfaced.

This was not compromise yet.

It was accommodation through inertia.

Then the signal appeared.

Not dramatically. Not as interruption.

An email arrived mid-morning, nested among routine correspondence. A project update. A location shift under discussion. A window opening in another city—temporary, contained, strategically useful. The kind of opportunity that had once activated him instantly.

He read it once, then again.

The timing worked. The rationale was clean. The move would make sense to anyone looking at the sequence of his work. It would not require explanation. It would preserve narrative coherence.

It was not urgent.

Which made it more dangerous.

Urgency forced decision. This did not. The window would remain open for a while. He could align schedules, make preliminary arrangements, leave without friction.

The exit was reasonable.

He did not feel pulled toward it.

That was new.

In the past, the availability of a clean exit had been enough. The logic of departure had always restored balance, even before action followed. Knowing he could leave was often as stabilizing as leaving itself.

Now, the knowledge sat inert.

He did not close the email.

He did not respond.

He left it where it was and continued with the day, noticing as he did that nothing in his immediate environment shifted to reflect the significance he would once have assigned to it.

The café filled and emptied. The woman appeared briefly in the afternoon, sat two tables away, worked, left. They exchanged no words. The continuity held.

By evening, Zeb realized something else.

He was no longer waiting for a moment that would clarify whether staying was intentional.

That moment was not coming.

The structure of the days had already answered the question— not with certainty, not with commitment, but with repetition that did not ask permission.

Staying had not been chosen.

But it was no longer provisional.

The exit remained available.

Clean. Logical. Uncontested.

And for the first time, Zeb understood that the cost ahead would not come from being trapped—

—but from discovering that freedom no longer automatically restored itself through motion.

The First Clean Exit

The next morning, Zeb opened the email again.

Not because he was undecided—because he was verifying that the door was real.

The message had not changed. The details were still clean. A location shift under discussion. A narrow window that aligned with his calendar more neatly than it had any right to. A flight route that existed without absurd layovers. A hotel option already vetted by someone who understood what he would and wouldn't tolerate. A local contact on the ground who would receive him without ceremony.

Nothing about it asked for improvisation.

It was the kind of exit his life had always rewarded.

He didn't tell anyone.

He didn't need to.

He set the phone down and crossed to the closet where his bag sat—still unpacked from his last move, as if his body had refused to declare arrival. He pulled it onto the bed and unzipped it without pausing.

The act didn't feel like betrayal.

It felt like alignment.

He started small.

A shirt folded into a rectangle. Socks rolled, then unrolled and folded again because he preferred them flat. Toiletries gathered without inventory. A charger. A small notebook. His passport checked once, then set on the nightstand where it could be reached without searching.

He wasn't packing a life.

He was packing a route.

The room stayed indifferent.

White walls. A narrow desk. A chair angled wrong. The same thin seam of light at the curtains' edge. No object in the space insisted on itself. Nothing looked back at him asking to be reconsidered.

He opened his laptop and pulled up flights.

The first option was workable. The second was better. A third appeared that was almost perfect—departing early enough to arrive before the afternoon heat thickened, late enough that he wouldn't have to perform urgency. A seat available in the section he preferred. A return ticket flexible enough to revise later.

He didn't book yet.

He didn't need the gesture of finality. He needed the confirmation that the exit could be clean.

He checked a map.

Routes from the airport. Transit options. A short list of contingencies. A local driver's number. He folded details into a sequence the way he always did—quietly, efficiently, reducing uncertainty without manufacturing control.

Then he opened his calendar.

The week ahead loosened easily. Calls could be moved. Meetings could be reframed as remote. Two obligations could be handed off without anyone panicking. One dinner invite—optional anyway—would disappear with a polite note.

He began drafting that note in his head and realized, with mild surprise, that he felt nothing about it.

No regret.

No pushback.

Just relief.

The relief didn't arrive with a rush. It arrived the way clean air arrives after leaving an over-managed room: not dramatic, just immediate, as if his nervous system recognized the register and stopped bracing.

Leaving would preserve everything he trusted.

Autonomy, intact.

Clarity, intact.

Narrative control—his most reliable form of safety—fully intact. No awkward escalation. No slow drift into implied meaning. No need to explain a relationship that had never asked to be named.

Most importantly: no need to risk disappointment.

The relief wasn't about escaping her.

It was about escaping the possibility of wanting more than the room had ever promised.

He sat with that for a moment, hands resting on the edge of the laptop.

He closed it—not decisively, just because the sequence was already known.

He showered quickly. Dressed. Went down to the street.

The café was open.

It always was.

The tables were arranged close together in their usual disorder. The radio playing too low to demand attention. A line at the counter that moved because it moved.

Zeb ordered coffee.

He took a stool near the interior wall because it was open.

He did not scan the room deliberately.

But he knew, almost immediately, that she wasn't there.

The plan did not include her or exclude her. It simply moved around the space where she might appear.

That, too, was a form of accounting.

He drank his coffee without being watched into coherence.

It was easier than he expected.

No tightening in his chest. No internal argument. No lingering sense of unfinished contact. The absence did not echo. The room simply held itself the way it always had, indifferent to the stories people brought into it.

He found himself thinking:

This is how it should feel when something matters less than motion.

The thought didn't carry cruelty.

It carried calibration.

He finished and left extra change without checking whether anyone saw.

Outside, the street took him.

He walked for an hour without destination, letting the city's noise do what silence couldn't: prevent him from rehearsing explanations.

Back in the room, he sat on the bed and looked at the bag.

Half-packed. Open. Waiting.

The exit remained perfectly available.

He could book the flight in under sixty seconds.

He could send the email. Confirm the route. Leave tomorrow or the next day. No one would stop him. No one would demand a conversation.

The cleanest kind of departure.

And still—he didn't book it.

Not because he chose to stay.

Not because he felt pulled.

Because there was no pressure yet.

The window was open. The door was real. The exit could remain an exit without becoming an act.

He zipped the bag halfway—not closing it, not leaving it fully exposed. A middle state. A posture that preserved option.

Then he set it back in the closet and left the door slightly ajar.

He did not feel conflicted.

He felt accurate.

The exit was still there.

And he would not pretend, yet, that not taking it meant anything.

Still—he stayed.

Constraint Without Demand

Zeb stayed.

Not in the way people usually meant it—not as a decision announced to himself, not as a posture taken against alternatives. He stayed because the day arrived and he did not interrupt it. Because the bag remained half-packed. Because the flight remained unbooked. Because nothing forced his hand.

But something had shifted.

Work adjusted first.

A call that would have required travel became remote without anyone objecting. A meeting shifted by a week, then by another. Each change justified easily by circumstances that did not require explanation. Someone suggested he remain available "for continuity," and the word landed differently now.

Continuity.

He agreed before examining why.

Another project extended itself—not formally, not ceremonially. Just an email that assumed his presence beyond the original scope. A revised timeline attached. A subtle expansion of responsibility. Nothing binding. Nothing dramatic.

He replied with a neutral acknowledgment.

That was all it took.

The system reorganized around his non-departure.

No one asked why he was still there.

No one thanked him for staying.

No one framed it as commitment.

The world simply treated his continued presence as fact and redistributed weight accordingly.

He felt it physically before he named it.

The days began to hold him differently.

Predictability settled in—not as comfort, not as confinement. As repetition that no longer refreshed itself. The café at similar hours. The same streets under slightly different light. The same conversations revisited with minor variations.

He had always relied on motion to reset the nervous system.

Now the reset did not arrive.

Even small departures—a long walk, a temporary trip for work—no longer dissolved the accumulation. He returned to the same baseline without the sensation of having exited anything.

Staying was no longer passive.

It had begun to generate structure.

He noticed a subtle recalibration in his professional instincts.

When new opportunities surfaced, he did not evaluate them solely on strategic merit. He measured them against disruption. Against continuity. Against whether departure would require explaining absence rather than simply enacting it.

That calculation was new.

He had once optimized for leverage.

Now he optimized for preservation of pattern.

He did not like recognizing that.

The bag remained in the closet, half-zipped. A gesture toward optionality.

But he stopped checking flights.

That, more than anything, marked the shift.

The exits had not disappeared.

He had stopped rehearsing them.

The cost began to show itself in small administrative ways.

He deferred tasks that would complicate staying. Accepted responsibilities that anchored him further into the week. Allowed projects to stretch rather than compress.

None of it felt dramatic.

It felt incremental.

That was what unsettled him.

Constraint without demand.

No one had asked him to stay.

No one had extracted a promise.

The woman had not altered her behavior in response to his continued presence. Some days they crossed paths in the café. Some days they did not. When they did, it remained unremarkable. When they didn't, nothing closed around the absence.

She remained what she had been: present without leverage.

That was precisely what made the narrowing unmistakable.

This was not attachment pulling him inward.

This was duration reducing the number of clean narratives available.

Another opportunity closed quietly.

Not because he declined it.

Because he did not pursue it quickly enough.

The window shifted. The timing misaligned. The clean exit lost its symmetry.

He noticed the change only after it had passed.

There was no regret.

There was no disappointment.

Only the factual recognition that staying had begun to eliminate the most elegant versions of departure.

He stood one evening at the waterfront, watching ferries move through their routes. Engines idling. Ropes tightening and releasing. Metal striking dock once, clean and dull.

He could still leave.

Nothing prevented it.

But leaving would now require explanation—not to her, not to colleagues.

To himself.

Why now?

Why after this long?

Why interrupt what had already demonstrated its capacity to hold?

The narrowing did not feel romantic.

It felt administrative.

He understood the distinction immediately.

If anything was forming, it wasn't longing. It was structure.

He had once believed freedom meant the ability to exit cleanly.

Now he understood something more exacting:

Freedom also meant the ability to remain without narrative.

And remaining had begun to cost him something he valued—

—not autonomy in theory—

—but the reflex of motion as self-restoration.

He did not resent the cost.

He did not elevate it.

He only recognized it.

Staying was no longer neutral.

And no one had needed to ask.

The Second Almost-Exit

The second opportunity arrived with authority.

Not tentative. Not exploratory.

It was framed.

A senior contact reached out directly—someone whose messages were never casual. The subject line was neutral. The body was concise. It referenced Zeb's prior work with precision: outcomes, not impressions. A defined role. A defined timeline. A city that would make sense in any retrospective account of his career.

Six to eight weeks on site.

Strategic visibility without theatrical exposure.

Influence without entanglement.

The kind of position people used later to explain why everything shifted upward from there.

He read it once.

Then again that night.

The terms held.

Compensation adjusted slightly above expectation. Housing pre-arranged. Travel simple. A team already briefed. They would prefer him in person.

The offer did not flatter.

It assumed.

Others noticed before he mentioned it.

On a call, a colleague said, almost casually, "That's strong. That's the right level for you right now." Another added, "If you're going to pivot, this is the clean way to do it."

Clean.

He understood what they meant.

This was not escape. It was trajectory.

Leaving now would not look like retreat.

It would look like momentum.

He could depart with structure. Notify the right people. Close out his current obligations cleanly. Re-enter motion with the legitimacy of advancement rather than the ambiguity of drift.

There would be no awkward silence.

No unanswered question about what had been forming here.

No need to test whether staying meant anything.

He would simply move.

The math was simple.

Leave now and preserve narrative coherence.

Stay, and the pattern would thicken further—harder to name, harder to defend.

He walked that evening without direction.

The waterfront opened and closed between buildings. Ferries moved without reference to him. The air carried salt and fuel, neither inviting nor resisting.

He felt relief when he imagined accepting.

Not excitement.

Relief.

Relief at the restoration of proportion.

Relief at not having to discover what staying required next.

He understood something then with uncomfortable clarity.

Leaving would preserve his preferred version of himself.

The man who exits before ambiguity hardens.

The man who moves before staying acquires consequence.

The man who never has to test whether continuity is chosen or simply endured.

He returned to his room and opened the message again.

His reply began easily.

Thank you. The timing aligns. I'm available.

He stopped typing.

He reread the line.

Nothing in it was false.

Nothing in it would damage anyone.

The woman did not factor into the decision in the way stories usually demanded. She had not positioned herself as reason or obstacle. She had not asked for time, or clarity, or intention.

If he left, she would not protest.

If he stayed, she would not claim it.

This was not about her.

It was about whether he would allow duration to become meaningful without guaranteeing that it would reward him.

He deleted the sentence.

He stood at the window.

Below, the city continued to move without consulting him. Deliveries unloaded. Lights shifted.

He recognized the hinge.

If he left now, he would be protecting something.

Not freedom.

Ease.

The ease of remaining untested by repetition.

The ease of never having to find out whether staying had substance or only inertia.

He sat back down.

This time he typed two sentences.

Appreciate the offer. The role makes sense.

Not this time.

No explanation.

No promise to revisit.

No softening language.

He hit send.

The response came an hour later.

Understood. Door remains open.

Of course it did.

The world did not punish refusal.

It adjusted.

The next morning he went to the café.

He did not open his laptop.

He sat with his coffee and let the room form around him.

The woman arrived later.

She took a table near the wall. Opened her notebook. Did not look toward him in any performative way.

Nothing in the room reflected what he had declined.

No music swelled.

No internal declaration formed.

He had not chosen her.

He had chosen exposure.

Exposure to staying without the guarantee that staying would justify itself.

Exposure to the possibility that continuity would produce nothing extraordinary at all.

That was the risk.

He felt no triumph.

No sacrifice.

Only the quiet awareness that he had stepped past a clean narrative and into something less legible.

The exits remained available.

But they no longer felt inevitable.

And for the first time, remaining required an active tolerance of uncertainty.

He drank his coffee slowly.

Across the room, she turned a page.

Nothing pressed.

Nothing resolved.

He stayed.

And this time, he knew he had.

Ordinary Disappointment

The failure was small enough to arrive without ceremony.

A meeting shifted earlier than expected. Not cancelled—just adjusted. A message sent, then clarified, then quietly superseded. The update landed somewhere between inboxes, caught by some and missed by others.

Zeb missed it.

He arrived twenty minutes late, the room already configured around decisions that did not require him. Voices low. Screens open. A chair scraped as he took the nearest seat. Someone nodded once. No one paused.

The meeting continued.

He tracked what had already been decided. Offered one correction near the end—precise, functional. It was acknowledged and folded in without discussion.

When it ended, no one lingered.

No reprimand. No recalibration. No scene.

The system had adjusted around his absence without friction.

That was the cost.

On the island, he had once left for less.

A business dinner that tightened too quickly—wine poured again before glasses were empty, voices lowering, the shift from negotiation into something more personal before he had agreed to it. A silence across the table that implied articulation was due. A look that suggested expectation forming faster than he could structure it.

He had booked a flight before morning.

Called it timing. Called it necessity.

Motion restored proportion. Distance restored control.

Here, nothing restored anything.

The day simply continued.

Later, at the café, the woman was already there.

She sat near the back wall, notebook open. She looked up when the door opened—not to greet him, but because the hinge made sound.

He took a stool at the counter.

After a while, she crossed the room with her cup and sat across from him—not ceremonially, not as inquiry. The seat was open. She used it.

"You were late today," she said.

Evenly. Not sharp. Not softened.

"Yes," Zeb said. "I missed a message."

She nodded. "It happens."

That was all.

She did not minimize it. Did not reinterpret it. Did not offer him a version of the story in which it meant less.

She let the moment remain intact.

He felt the exposure settle—not as shame, not as humiliation.

As accuracy.

A small diminishment that did not escalate. A correction that did not justify reaction. A fact that would have once triggered departure simply because departure was available.

In the past, he would have converted this into motion.

Scheduled something elsewhere.

Booked a flight under the language of alignment.

Reframed the day as misplacement rather than error.

Now it remained.

The system had not punished him. It had functioned.

The woman returned to her notebook. No emotional labor was extended to absorb his discomfort. No demand was made of him either.

The room resumed its ordinary scale.

He watched a condensation ring form beneath his glass and fade as the wood absorbed it.

This was what staying exposed him to.

Not betrayal. Not rupture.

Ordinary diminishment.

Being present when the day did not arrange itself around him—and not leaving because of it.

She finished her coffee first.

"I'll see you later," she said.

Not promise. Not assumption.

Continuation.

"Okay," he replied.

She left.

He remained seated.

No motion to convert the moment. No distance to clean it.

Only the quiet fact of having been present—and imperfect— without retreat.

And this, more than the missed meeting, marked the shift.

He had chosen exposure.

Now he was inside it.

The Reflex

Two evenings later, the day finished without punctuation and Zeb found himself walking toward the café as if confirming a habit rather than choosing one. The awareness came with him—not expectation, not anticipation—just the small new fact that had begun to appear in his thinking before he could screen it:

She might be there.

He told himself it did not matter. And that was almost true.

The café was in its in-between hour. Not crowded, not quiet. People sat longer than necessary because leaving required decision. Cups moved. Chairs scraped once and were corrected. The radio held a thin station that never fully became music.

She was near the window, reading.

A strand of hair slipped forward and she tucked it behind her ear without interrupting the line of her gaze. The movement wasn't made for anyone. It was simply upkeep.

The room was shallow enough that the counter and the window shared the same narrow wall of air.

Zeb ordered coffee and took his usual position at the counter. He did not look at her again immediately, but in a space this small, peripheral vision was sufficient—the turn of a page, the pause between lines, the absence of any posture meant to be read.

After a few minutes, something ordinary passed between them—

"It's cooler today."

"Yeah. The wind shifted."

That was enough.

The words settled and stayed where they landed. Neither of them extended it.

And still, he could have told her.

About the offer. About the city he had declined. About the six or eight weeks that would have preserved his pattern.

The thought surfaced cleanly, the way logistics always surfaced in him—without romance, without dramatic framing. He saw the sentence in his mind as if he had already written it:

I was offered something elsewhere.

He imagined her response—not emotional, just legible. A neutral curiosity, maybe a brief nod of approval. A small confirmation that leaving remained normal.

He imagined the rest of it too: packing without hesitation. The exit restoring proportion. The nervous system returning to the register it trusted.

The sequence arranged itself easily.

He said nothing.

Not because she would have stopped him. Not because she had asked him to stay. Because saying it would have acknowledged—quietly, irreversibly—that she now existed inside the calculation.

That was the narrowing.

He drank his coffee. The bitterness registered more strongly than usual, as if his body had begun to notice flavor when it could not solve the day through motion. A page lifted and settled near the window.

What was being exchanged came into focus—not as philosophy, as sensation:

Not freedom for attachment. Freedom for continuity.

The ability to reset through departure—thinning. The reflex to leave cleanly—slowing.

He did not resent it. He did not romanticize it. But he felt it now in his body as a slight resistance where certainty used to sit—at the base of the throat, just above the sternum, a place that had always loosened when a flight became real.

Leaving would still be possible. But it would no longer be neutral.

He finished his coffee more slowly than he needed to. He stood, left change without checking whether anyone saw, and stepped back into the street.

At the corner, he glanced through the glass.

She lifted her cup. Her eyes met his for a fraction—not long enough to establish meaning, not long enough to become signal—only long enough to confirm recognition.

Then she looked away and returned to her page as if nothing had occurred.

The exit had been clean. The refusal had been clean. The narrowing was not.

And for the first time, Zeb understood that what was closing wasn't geography.

It was reflex.

End State: Constraint Accepted

The next day moved forward without adjustment.

Zeb worked.

Not differently than he had the day before, or the week before that. Documents revised. Messages answered. Timelines confirmed and revised again. Nothing urgent surfaced. Nothing resolved itself cleanly. The work occupied the hours it was given and no more.

He sat at a narrow table near the back of the café, the chair angled slightly wrong for comfort but usable if one didn't insist on correcting it. He left it as it was. His bag rested at his feet. The laptop woke, hummed faintly, then went quiet.

The woman was there for part of the afternoon.

Not seated with him. Not apart from him in any meaningful way. She occupied the room the way others did—present, functional, unconcerned with whether the overlap mattered.

At one point she passed behind him to return a cup to the counter. He registered the movement without turning.

Later, she was gone.

This time he noticed.

Not as loss. As subtraction.

The space she had occupied did not close around itself. It did not echo. It simply remained open—an ordinary vacancy that would once have triggered calculation: how long until the pattern changes, how much meaning is being assigned, what needs to be managed.

He did not manage it.

His attention returned to the page in front of him. He corrected a line that had bothered him for days—not because it now made sense, but because it no longer needed to be perfect. He left another unresolved and moved on.

He noticed that he was no longer optimizing.

That, more than anything, marked the shift.

This was the alignment. Not clarity. Not fulfillment.

Constraint.

The freedom to leave remained intact in theory. He could still see exits when he chose to look for them. Travel would still be possible. Offers would still arrive shaped cleanly enough to justify motion.

What had changed was not availability.

It was relevance.

Leaving would now require an answer—not to her, not to colleagues—to himself.

Why now? Why after this long? Why interrupt what had already demonstrated its capacity to hold?

He felt the narrowing not as drama but as embodiment: a mild compression beneath the ribs; a slower sweep of attention across the room; a small, factual knowledge that if he left, he would feel the absence of this table, this street, this repetition.

And that feeling would belong to him.

There had been a time when he would have left the second he sensed himself settling.

He stayed.

When the work reached its natural stopping point—not finished, just sufficient—Zeb closed the laptop and slid it into his bag. He did not leave immediately. He sat for another minute, hands resting on the table, gaze unfixed.

He let the discomfort of remaining register without solving it.

Near the counter, someone laughed once and stopped. A chair wobbled and was corrected. The radio fell into static for half a second and returned. Nothing in the room bent toward significance.

Then—briefly—the woman returned.

Only long enough to retrieve something forgotten: a pen, a folded paper, something small and necessary. She crossed the room without scanning it, as if her attention had already been assigned elsewhere.

At the doorway, she glanced back—not searching.

Their eyes met.

Not long enough to establish meaning. Long enough to confirm recognition.

No smile. No signal. No invitation to interpret.

Then she left.

This time, Zeb felt the narrowing.

Not attachment.

Accountability.

He had stayed through enough days that departure would now create a small tear in continuity. No one would name it.

But he would.

He stood.

At the counter, he returned his cup himself. He wiped a small spill with a napkin and set it aside. The action was minor, unremarkable, complete.

Outside, the street took him back without pause.

Nothing had been resolved. Nothing had been secured. Nothing had been promised.

But something had been accepted.

The day continued. And Zeb continued within it—limited, exposed, narrowed—not as escape, not as sacrifice, but as the quiet acceptance of a life that no longer reset itself through motion.

He no longer required a clean exit to remain intact.

He required the discipline to stay.

And for the first time, that discipline did not feel temporary.

What He Could Not Read

That evening, the café was half-full.

Not crowded. Not quiet. The in-between hour when people sat longer than necessary because leaving required decision. The air carried coffee gone bitter and something fried from down the street. Outside, the light had thinned but not yet surrendered.

Zeb took a table near the back.

She was already there.

Not close. Not distant. Two tables away, angled slightly toward the open front. A notebook in front of her. A cup nearly empty. Her bag on the chair beside her.

Nothing in her posture suggested waiting.

He ordered coffee. Sat. Opened his laptop without turning it on.

She checked her phone.

It was a small movement. Ordinary.

Her expression did not change dramatically. No visible reaction. No flinch. No visible disappointment or relief. But something in the line of her shoulders shifted—almost imperceptibly—like a structure redistributing weight.

She read once. Then again.

The phone remained in her hand longer than usual. She did not type immediately. Instead, she placed it face down on the table and looked outward through the open front—not at anything specific. Not at the water. Not at the people moving past. Just outward.

Still.

Zeb watched without meaning to. He tried to place the register of it.

It was not distress. Not distraction. Not anticipation.

The room continued around her. A chair scraped. Someone laughed too loudly and corrected themselves. The radio slipped into static for half a second and returned.

She picked up the phone again.

Typed something brief. Stopped. Deleted it.

Typed again. Sent.

Then she closed her notebook without marking her place.

That was new.

She never closed it mid-page.

She slid the pen into the spine and rested her hands on the cover for a moment as if steadying something internal—something not meant to be seen, not meant to be offered.

No one else in the café noticed.

Zeb realized he was leaning forward slightly. He corrected himself, shifting back in the chair as if distance could restore the old rules.

She stood.

Not abruptly. Not ceremonially.

She placed money on the table, gathered her bag, and walked toward the door without scanning the room.

She did not look at him.

Not pointedly. Simply not at all.

The door opened. Closed.

The space she had occupied remained unchanged: the chair slightly angled; the faint ring of the cup still on the wood.

Zeb waited for the internal reset that usually followed such moments.

It did not arrive.

He could not categorize what he had seen.

It had not been vulnerability. It had not been indifference. It had not been performance.

It had been something lived through and absorbed.

He had no language for it.

For a brief second, a thought moved through him without framing:

I don't know what that cost her.

The sentence did not expand. It did not resolve.

The café resumed its ordinary rhythm.

Zeb opened his laptop and stared at the blank screen.

For the first time since staying had begun to take shape, he felt the thin edge of something unfamiliar—not fear, not jealousy, not even concern.

Opacity.

He closed the laptop again.

The exits still existed.

But the map no longer felt complete.

He finished his coffee. Left extra change as usual. Stepped into the street.

The city moved as it always had.

And for the first time, remaining felt less like accuracy—and more like exposure to something he could not pre-read.

He walked without deciding where.

A ferry horn sounded once, distant and indifferent.

It did not clarify anything.

CHAPTER 15

The Risk of Being Seen

They had drifted farther down the waterfront this time. Not by plan, not by suggestion—just a slight adjustment in route that placed them inside a smaller café open on two sides, its tables arranged more for traffic than conversation.

They were already there.

Not seated together in a way that implied intention—just occupying adjacent space that had not yet sorted itself into categories. The hour sat between uses: too late for morning urgency, too early for the afternoon's compression. People came and went without pattern.

Zeb had a notebook open in front of him. It was not full. He had written a few lines earlier and then stopped, not because he was finished, but because the need to continue had not arrived. The pen rested across the page, angled slightly away from his hand. He did not cap it.

Across from him—not directly opposite, not aligned—the woman worked on something small and bounded. A stack of papers folded once, then unfolded again. She read, marked a line, set the page aside. Her movements were economical, not optimized. Nothing in them suggested she was aware of being observed.

The table was too narrow to divide cleanly. Their belongings touched the same surface without encroachment. A phone vibrated briefly and was silenced without apology. Outside, a muffled announcement drifted across the water, distant enough to register as texture rather than interruption.

Zeb noticed that he had not oriented himself toward her.

Not physically. Not attentively.

This was unusual enough to register, but not enough to provoke correction. His posture remained neutral—spine upright, shoulders unheld. He was not angling for space. He was not closing it off either.

The café held.

Cups landed and left again. A chair scraped once and stopped.

Zeb read a line in his notebook again. It did not require revision. He left it as it was. He became aware that he wasn't scanning the room.

The small readiness he usually carried—the habit of mapping exits and calibrating tone—was simply not there.

He did not feel exposed.

He did not feel hidden.

Across the table, the woman turned a page. The sound was small, nearly lost in the room. She paused, pen hovering, then made a note in the margin. Zeb did not read it. He did not try to.

Outside, a gull dropped something hard onto the pavement and startled itself. A man near the door stood and left without finishing his drink. No one remarked on it.

Zeb's phone buzzed once. He glanced, then set it down again. Whatever it wanted could wait.

He noticed that speaking would cost less than usual. Not because he wanted to talk—because nothing in the room would demand repayment.

The woman looked up from her papers briefly—not at him, exactly, but toward the center of the room. She adjusted her chair a few inches, aligning it with the table's edge, then returned to her work.

Zeb shifted his pen slightly. The movement was unconscious.

"I might head out later than planned," he said.

The sentence entered the space without preface. It was not aimed. It did not seek response. It was accurate, but not explanatory.

She glanced at him briefly, just long enough to register content.

"Okay," she said. No question followed.

She returned to the page in front of her.

The room absorbed the exchange without altering its rhythm. A cup was set down nearby. Someone stood and reached for a jacket. A ramp thudded into place, closer this time, then the sound receded.

He turned another page in his notebook. The next space was blank. He did not fill it.

The woman gathered her papers into a neat stack and slid them into her bag. The gesture suggested pause rather than departure. She set the bag back down at her feet and reached for her cup.

"This place stays usable longer than most," she said, looking toward the open front of the café. "People don't rush you out."

Zeb nodded. "It helps," he said.

He did not elaborate. She did not ask what it helped with.

They sat again without speaking.

Zeb noticed that his breathing remained even. His jaw was loose. The small readiness he often carried—the sense that he should be prepared to disengage cleanly—was absent. He did not attribute meaning to that absence. He simply registered it.

A server passed behind them and cleared an empty plate from a neighboring table. The sound of it leaving registered more than its arrival.

Zeb wrote a single word in the margin of his notebook and closed it. He did not tuck it away. It remained where it was, visible but inactive.

The woman checked her watch and then did nothing about it.

Outside, a ferry docked. People stepped off and dispersed without hesitation, already moving toward other obligations. The café did not respond.

Zeb felt no pull toward departure. He also felt no need to stay. The interval held.

Whatever speech might come later—if it came at all—would not be the result of pressure. He understood that without naming it. The environment had done its work simply by not asking.

He took a sip of water. Set the glass down.

The room continued.

The First Unmanaged Sentence

The café shifted around them without changing.

A group came in and immediately rearranged themselves— chairs moved, a table pulled closer to the wall, voices lowered not out of courtesy but because the room required it. A server navigated the congestion with practiced indifference. Outside, the water kept moving, ferries arriving and leaving on a schedule that did not care who was watching.

Zeb had his phone out now, not scrolling, just reading something once, then again, as if repetition might change the content. He set it down beside the notebook and didn't touch it.

The woman returned from the counter with a small glass of tea. She did not offer to bring him anything. She sat and placed the glass carefully near the edge of the table, angled so it wouldn't be knocked by someone passing too close.

She looked at his phone, not the screen—just the presence of it.

"Do you need to answer that?" she asked.

It was practical. Not concern. Not permission. The kind of question that belonged to logistics.

"No," Zeb said. "Not yet."

She nodded once and took a sip of the tea. The liquid was hot enough that she held it for a moment before swallowing, then set it down again.

Outside, a horn sounded and cut off mid-note. Something metallic clattered at the curb—delivery cart, loose chain, a wheel striking a seam in the stone. It smoothed out and continued.

Zeb picked up his pen, turned it once between his fingers, then set it down again.

"Are you heading to the site after this?" she asked.

He understood what she meant by site without needing to. He had said it once earlier, days ago, as a word with no biography attached. It had stayed that way.

"In a bit," he said.

She stirred the tea with a small spoon, not because it needed stirring but because the motion occupied her hand. She stopped when the spoon began to click against the glass.

"Is it always that kind of work?" she asked. "The type that doesn't really end?"

Again—practical. A remark about shape, not content. She didn't ask what he was building, or for whom, or where the money came from. The question landed where it could land without turning into invitation.

"Usually," Zeb said.

He paused long enough that it could have become something else—an opening, a turn.

It didn't.

The room moved on.

A couple at the next table argued quietly about directions. The words were soft but tense, the kind of disagreement that was less about maps than about fatigue. Someone behind the counter dropped a spoon and didn't apologize, just picked it up and continued.

Zeb looked through the open front at the street, watching the uneven waves of foot traffic loosen and tighten around the corner. He did not evaluate faces. He did not take inventory.

"I don't usually stay this long," he said.

The sentence fell out cleanly, not breathless, not weighted. It was simple enough to sound like scheduling.

He did not attach explanation.

He did not convert it into a story about restlessness or fear. He did not qualify it with a laugh or soften it into charm. The sentence just existed.

He realized he had said it only after it was already in the air.

The woman did not look at him. Not pointedly. Not avoiding. She kept her eyes on the tea, on the glass, on the spoon resting on the saucer.

She nodded once.

And that was all.

No follow-up. No "why." No "where do you go."

No interest packaged as curiosity.

She let it stand as a fact the way she had let other facts stand—unclaimed, unfiled.

Zeb felt something in his chest register, not as relief, not as threat. More like a small recalibration: a system expecting cost and finding none.

He picked up his water and drank. The glass was half empty and stayed that way.

Outside, a fresh wave of pedestrians reached the curb and broke apart, their pace quickening once they cleared the crosswalk. The café absorbed a few of them; the rest kept moving.

The woman checked her watch.

"I should go soon," she said, not as departure ritual—just as placement.

Zeb nodded. "Yeah."

She gathered her bag with the same economy she always used, strap over shoulder, phone in hand, tea left half finished without apology. She stood, paused long enough to glance once toward the door, then stepped into the street and was absorbed by it.

Zeb remained. Not to make a point. Not to preserve anything.

The table in front of him held only his notebook, his phone, his water. Ordinary objects. Ordinary weight.

He let it stay unsorted.

The room continued, indifferent and sufficient, and his body stayed where it was without tension—exposed by one small accuracy, and untouched by consequence.

Fragment Without Context

Another day, further down the waterfront, they left at the same time and found themselves moving in the same direction without having agreed to.

The street ran along the water here, wide enough to accommodate walkers without turning into a promenade. Stone underfoot, worn smooth in places where people tended to slow without realizing it. The ferries moved in and out at irregular intervals, their engines audible but not dominant, sound folding into the city rather than announcing itself.

Zeb carried a thin folder under his arm. Papers he needed later, nothing urgent enough to demand attention now. The woman walked a half-step behind him, then drifted forward again when the path narrowed. Neither adjusted pace deliberately. Their bodies handled it.

They did not talk at first.

Not because silence had been chosen. There was simply nothing pressing itself forward. A cyclist passed too close, rang a bell that sounded more irritated than warning, and was gone. Someone shouted from a boat moored along the quay; the reply came back delayed and indistinct.

Zeb noticed, distantly, that his shoulders stayed where they were. No tightening when she came closer. No release when she fell back. His attention stayed wide, distributed across movement, sound, surface.

At a low stone wall near the water, she stopped to check something in her bag. Zeb paused a few feet ahead without thinking, then turned and leaned against the railing, giving her space without staging it.

She sorted papers quickly—tickets, a folded map, something handwritten—then tucked them back in. The movement was efficient, practiced. She looked up only when she was finished.

"Did you want to keep going?" she asked.

"Sure," Zeb said.

They resumed.

The question hadn't carried weight. It hadn't been an invitation dressed up as politeness. Just confirmation of direction.

They walked another block before Zeb spoke again.

"I don't like meetings that pretend to be conversations," he said.

The sentence arrived with no lead-in.

He didn't look at her when he said it. He watched the water instead, the way light broke unevenly across its surface, the faint oil sheen near the docks catching and releasing color.

It wasn't an explanation. It wasn't framed as complaint. It was an observation, clean and bounded.

She nodded once.

"That makes sense," she said.

No elaboration. No curiosity about which meetings, or who staged them, or why he'd brought it up now. She accepted the sentence for what it was—a description of constraint, not an opening.

They walked.

A man stood near the edge of the quay feeding something to birds that were too cautious to approach. He threw bread anyway, more out of habit than expectation. The birds circled, landed farther down, ignored him.

Zeb felt the echo of the sentence register internally—not as exposure, not as risk. He wasn't waiting for something to follow it. His body didn't brace the way it used to after saying things that edged too close to truth.

That was new.

Normally, after saying something even mildly revealing, he tracked impact reflexively: did it land, did it shift tone, did it create obligation. Here, there was nothing to track. The sentence had entered the space and then settled, unclaimed.

They stopped at a pedestrian crossing where the light took longer than necessary to change. Cars idled, engines vibrating faintly through the ground. Someone tapped a foot impatiently nearby.

The woman glanced at the light, then back toward the water.

"I have a deadline this afternoon," she said. "It's flexible, but not generous."

Zeb nodded. "Those are the worst kind."

She smiled briefly—not amused, just recognizing the shape of the thing.

The light changed. They crossed.

On the other side, the street narrowed again, forcing them into closer alignment. Zeb shifted the folder under his arm without breaking stride. She adjusted her bag to her other shoulder. The movements overlapped without coordination.

Another fragment surfaced in Zeb—not premeditated, not pressing.

"I don't explain my work unless I have to," he said.

It wasn't defensive. It wasn't proud. It was simply a line he lived by, stated without ornament.

She considered that for half a second.

"That probably saves time," she said.

"Yes," Zeb replied.

And that was the end of it.

No inquiry into what the work was. No implication that explanation would be welcomed or withheld. She responded to the content of the sentence, not the boundary it implied.

They reached a point where the street angled away from the water. The sound of engines softened. The city resumed a more enclosed rhythm—voices bouncing between buildings, footsteps sharper on stone.

Zeb noticed, again, the absence of aftermath.

He was not replaying what he'd said. He was not waiting for a question that would require him to defend or expand. His breath stayed even. His attention stayed outward.

It wasn't closeness. It was permission.

They slowed near a storefront where someone was rearranging chairs for later, stacking them with care that suggested the task mattered to him even if no one noticed. One small table wobbled; he corrected it with a folded napkin under the leg and moved on.

The woman stopped there.

"I need to turn back," she said. "I've got about an hour before things pile up."

Zeb nodded. "I've got a few calls to make."

Neither of them framed it as leaving the other.

They stood for a moment, bodies angled toward different directions, the pause practical rather than weighted. Zeb was aware of the fragments he had offered—not as disclosures, but as coordinates. He felt no urge to add another to balance them out.

"See you around," she said.

"Yeah," Zeb said. "See you."

She turned and walked back the way they'd come. Zeb watched her for a step or two, then turned in the opposite direction and kept moving.

As he walked, he noticed the difference clearly.

Nothing had been extracted.

Nothing had been stored for later use.

The fragments he had spoken did not pull at him. They did not ask to be integrated into a narrative. They existed where they had been said, complete in their incompleteness.

Zeb adjusted the folder under his arm and continued on, the city closing around him in its ordinary way.

Not openness.

Precision.

The Withheld Question

They were back at the café without having returned together.

Zeb arrived first this time, took the same stool near the counter, set his bag beneath his feet. He ordered coffee and waited. The room was fuller than earlier in the day, but not crowded—people cycling through, coats draped over chairs, conversations overlapping without needing coherence.

She came in several minutes later, phone in hand, reading as she walked. She ordered tea, nodded to the server, and took the seat beside him as if it had remained open for her.

No greeting ritual.
No acknowledgment of sequence.

She set the phone face down and let out a single, quiet exhale—administrative, not emotional.

Zeb registered her presence as density, not alert. His shoulders stayed loose.

They sat without speaking.

Outside, rain had started—not enough to dramatize the street, just enough to darken the stone and change the sound. Footsteps softened. Traffic slowed. Someone snapped an umbrella too close to the doorway and was corrected by a look from the server, nothing more.

She stirred her tea, stopped when the spoon clicked, then wrapped her hands around the glass.

"That meeting you mentioned earlier," she said, still looking outward, "did it end the way you expected?"

It was a real opening—clean, usable. Zeb felt it immediately. He could answer in logistics. He could offer context. He could give her something that would make the question feel finished.

"No," he said. "It rarely does."

She nodded once.

The pause that followed had shape.

There was room for the second question—the one that would turn "meeting" into content, consequence, biography. Zeb knew that rhythm intimately. He had lived inside rooms where silence was treated as waste and curiosity as entitlement.

She did not take the room.

She lifted the tea, winced faintly at the heat, set it down again.

"That makes sense," she said.

And then she let it stop.

Zeb felt the absence register, not as comfort but as exposure. The withheld question had weight—not because it accused him, but because it refused to define him. It left his answer where it was, unprocessed.

He realized he had been bracing for follow-up.

Not consciously. The body did it on its own: a small tightening behind the sternum, the reflex to abstract, to reframe, to manage what "no" might invite.

Nothing arrived.

The readiness had nowhere to go.

Outside, the rain thickened slightly, droplets tracing loose paths down the glass. A man near the window raised his phone, took a picture of the street, and put it away without looking at it.

Zeb drank his coffee.

The absence of interrogation did not feel like safety. It felt like risk.

If she had asked more, he would have known how to respond. He would have stayed inside familiar constraints—information paced, disclosure controlled. Her restraint removed the rails without pushing him forward.

He was exposed without being cornered.

She adjusted the strap of her bag with one hand, the movement casual and finished.

"I've got about ten minutes," she said. "Then I need to head out."

Zeb nodded. "Same."

They did not use the time as a container that needed filling.

A server passed behind them and refilled Zeb's cup without asking. Zeb moved his elbow out of the way. He noticed that she did not track the exchange. She didn't watch him be serviced. She didn't file it as social information.

That mattered.

He felt the earlier fragments he'd offered over the last few days hover at the edge of awareness—separate points, intact. None of them had been pulled on. None had been tested.

He understood, with a clarity that didn't need interpretation: the restraint was hers, but the risk was his.

She had left a door unlocked without inviting him through it.

The rain eased. Someone pushed the door open with their shoulder, shaking water from their coat, apologizing too much. The apology was waved away.

The woman checked her watch and stood, sliding the strap back into place.

"I'll see you later," she said—not promise, not plan. Orientation.

"Yeah," Zeb said. "Later."

She left.

Zeb stayed.

He didn't replay the exchange. He sat with the shape of what hadn't been asked—the way it widened him instead of narrowing him.

For the first time, he understood something cleanly:

Being known didn't always advance through inquiry. Sometimes it advanced through restraint.

He picked up his bag, stepped outside as the rain tapered off, and let the city take him back without ceremony.

The risk remained.

Not as threat.

As possibility.

Naming Without Claim

They were sitting on a low wall near the water, not oriented toward the view so much as accommodated by it. The stone held the day's warmth unevenly. Zeb shifted once, found a cooler patch, and stayed. The woman sat a short distance away—close enough to share the space, far enough that neither had to adjust.

A ferry passed without stopping, engines low, wake spreading and then dissolving against the edge. The sound carried briefly and folded back into the city.

She checked something on her phone—not reading, just confirming—and slid it into her bag. Her hands settled on the strap, fingers hooked loosely as if to keep it from tipping.

"I might be gone next week," she said. "Or not. It depends on how things line up."

Zeb nodded. "That tracks."

She glanced at him once, then back to the water. "You move around a lot," she said.

It wasn't a question. It wasn't framed for response. It was an observation assembled from fragments, not curiosity.

"Enough," Zeb said.

The word stood without reinforcement.

They let it.

Nearby, a man argued into a headset, voice pitched just high enough to carry. He walked in short loops, stopping and starting, repeating the same phrase with minor variation. No one intervened. No one listened.

She leaned back slightly, palms flat against the stone, redistributing her weight. "I used to think staying was the harder choice," she said. "I'm not sure that's true anymore."

Zeb didn't meet the sentence. He watched the water work against the edge, the way it never quite repeated itself.

When he spoke, it wasn't reply so much as alignment.

"I tend to leave before things settle."

The phrase arrived whole.

He didn't explain it or qualify it. He named it and left it where it was.

She didn't look at him. Not to avoid. Not to measure. Her attention stayed on the water, where a thin line of light broke and reformed with each small wave.

"Mm," she said.

No reassurance. No counterexample. No attempt to stabilize what the sentence implied.

The statement remained what it was: a description without demand, a boundary without claim.

Zeb felt the difference register—not relief, but exposure. In other rooms, a sentence like that would have been redirected, turned into something easier to hold.

Here, it stayed where it landed.

A gull dropped onto the railing a few feet away, watched them briefly, then hopped down and disappeared. The air carried fuel and salt.

She shifted again, settling back against the stone. "I'm bad at endings," she said. "I usually miss them."

Zeb nodded once.

He didn't mirror it. He didn't trade disclosures. He didn't reach for symmetry.

"I don't plan exits," he said. "I recognize them."

That was all.

The words didn't tighten around him. He didn't feel the reflex to track how they landed, or to buffer them with something easier to hold.

She received the sentence the way she had received the others—by not converting it.

"That's efficient," she said.

"Yes," Zeb replied.

The city continued.

Someone laughed behind them, sharp and brief. A bike rattled past on uneven stone. The ferry's wake reached the wall and receded, leaving the surface nearly unchanged.

They sat without speaking.

The sentences he had named did not accumulate. They stayed separate—accurate, unclaimed.

When she stood, it was with the same economy as always. She brushed dust from her palms, slung her bag over her shoulder, checked the time without apology.

"I've got to go," she said.

"Yeah," Zeb said.

They didn't mark the exchange. Nothing had reached completion or been deferred. She walked along the water, pace steady, absorbed into the city without friction.

Zeb stayed for another minute, then stood and went the opposite direction.

As he walked, he noticed the absence of a familiar residue—the impulse to revise how his words might now live inside someone else.

Nothing had been taken or corrected.

What remained were facts he could continue to live inside—spoken once, intact.

The Risk Registers

The day thinned without announcing itself.

Zeb walked alone for a while after leaving the water, not away from her and not toward anything else. The city adjusted around him—streets narrowing, sound changing texture, light losing its edge as afternoon folded into something less directive.

He stopped once to let a delivery truck back into a space that was too small for it. The driver leaned out the window, gestured, corrected, tried again. Zeb waited without irritation, weight settled evenly through his feet. When the truck finally cleared the curb, he crossed without hurry.

Silence followed him.

Not the kind that needed to be protected. Not the kind that asked to be interpreted. It arrived because nothing pressed against it.

He noticed his breath first. Not its depth or rhythm—only that it wasn't being managed. It moved without supervision.

His shoulders stayed where they were.

That was new.

Normally, after saying something accurate, his body tightened before his thoughts did—preparing to compensate for what had been exposed. The reflex was automatic, reliable.

It did not activate.

He adjusted the strap of his bag on his shoulder, more from habit than necessity, and kept walking. The movement didn't correct anything. It didn't re-establish distance. It didn't close him back down.

The exposure remained. Not charged. Not demanding. Just present.

The world felt more precisely bounded. Distances resolved cleanly. His body occupied its space without spillover.

He passed the café without stopping.

The stools were mostly empty now. Someone was wiping the counter, movements methodical, unhurried. The radio played at the same low volume as always. The room did not register him.

That mattered.

He kept going.

At a corner near the water, he leaned briefly against a railing worn smooth by hands that had paused there for reasons unrelated to him. The surface was cool. He rested his palms flat against it and stood that way for a moment—not to ground himself, not to think, simply because the posture presented itself.

The water moved below, indifferent and continuous.

The risk settled into his body—not as danger, but as a recalibrated baseline. Something had shifted from defense to discernment.

He was not more open. He was more exact.

Trust did not feel expansive. It felt narrowing.

The reduction did not weaken him. It constrained him into accuracy.

He straightened, adjusted his stance, and stepped back into the street. A cyclist cut across his path; Zeb slowed without annoyance and continued. Someone brushed past him without apology. He did not register it as intrusion.

The silence moved with him, but it did not follow him inward. It thinned when the street grew louder. It did not take up residence in his head.

Later, back in his room, he set his bag down and washed his hands. The water ran clear. He dried them and stood for a moment without sitting, without reaching for his phone.

Nothing needed checking. Nothing needed securing.

He sat on the edge of the bed and felt the day close around itself. The fragments he had offered over the last few days— sentences, observations, boundaries—did not assemble into a story. They did not ask to be reconciled.

They had already done their work.

Zeb lay back and let his eyes close.

The risk remained. Not as threat. Not as promise.

As orientation.

Being seen accurately, incompletely, without capture did not dissolve him.

It narrowed him.

Sleep later came without ceremony, carrying no residue—only the quiet precision of a body no longer bracing against what had already been allowed.

Asymmetry Maintained

They crossed paths again without planning it.

Late afternoon had thinned the city's edges. The light came in at a lower angle now, slipping between buildings rather than flattening them. Zeb was standing near a corner kiosk, scanning a short list on his phone—nothing urgent, just enough to orient the rest of the day—when he felt the familiar shift in density beside him.

She was already there, waiting for the same signal to cross. A small bag at her feet, jacket unzipped, posture neutral. She looked toward the street, not at him.

They nodded once.

Not greeting. Not recognition. Placement.

The light took longer than expected. Traffic stalled and then lurched forward again. Someone behind them sighed loudly, then stopped.

She broke the pause first.

"I'm heading out of town tomorrow," she said. "Just for a few days."

The statement landed without framing. Not announcement. Not invitation. The kind of information that belonged to logistics rather than intimacy.

Zeb nodded. "Okay."

She glanced at him briefly, then back to the street. "I've got a project that needs hands-on time. Remote doesn't work for it."

"That makes sense," he said.

She shifted her weight slightly, the strap of her bag sliding along her shoulder. "It's not far," she added, then stopped herself. The sentence didn't complete. It didn't need to.

Zeb felt the familiar shape of an opening appear—the moment where reciprocity was usually expected. He could have offered something parallel: where he'd be, when he was leaving next, what obligations waited for him. The rhythm of exchange was well known to him. He'd mastered it early.

He did nothing.

Not out of restraint. Out of clarity.

The information she'd offered didn't require balancing. It didn't pull on him. It wasn't a bid for symmetry.

He let it remain hers.

The light changed. They crossed.

On the other side, the street narrowed. They slowed naturally, walking a few steps together before their paths angled apart. Zeb adjusted his pace to avoid colliding with someone coming the opposite direction. She stepped around a puddle without comment.

"I'll see you when I'm back," she said—not as plan, not as promise. Just orientation again.

"Yeah," Zeb said. "Take care."

She nodded once and turned down a side street without looking back. The movement was clean, unhesitant.

Zeb continued straight.

He noticed, as he walked, the absence of a familiar sensation—the subtle pressure to return what had been offered. He didn't feel unbalanced. He didn't feel as though something was pending. The asymmetry sat exactly where it belonged.

Later, he passed the café again.

The stools were occupied by different people now, bodies leaning into conversations that seemed louder than necessary. A server moved between tables with practiced neutrality. The room held no memory of earlier days.

Zeb didn't stop.

He kept walking, the city rearranging itself around him, and understood with quiet certainty that something important had been preserved.

What was shared stayed where it was given.
It didn't convert.

He had not been drawn into symmetry as proof of trust.

The balance remained intact—not because it had been negotiated, but because it had not been disturbed.

And that, he recognized without elevation, was what allowed trust to continue without distortion.

CHAPTER 16

The House Revisited

Z eb had not planned to return. The island arranged it the way it arranged most things—through access rather than invitation. A meeting shifted earlier. A call resolved itself without requiring him in person. The calendar opened just enough to make the drive practical.

The road narrowed as it left the mainland.

Commercial edges gave way to marsh. The air shifted from exhaust to salt and low vegetation. Ahead, the bridge appeared—steel truss rising modestly over the channel, its frame a darkened lattice against the sky.

It had been there for more than a century.

Built originally for freight—timber, citrus, shipments that no longer moved that way. Repurposed, reinforced, maintained. The rivets remained visible along the beams, slightly irregular, hammered in by hands that assumed permanence without imagining the present configuration.

The tires met metal.

The first contact produced a hollow, percussive rhythm—rubber against plated steel. The sound traveled up through the chassis and into the steering column, faint vibration registering in his palms. The bridge did not attempt silence. It announced crossing through sound.

The gridwork beneath the tires created a steady pattern—measured, mechanical, almost metronomic. The car's engine lowered itself to match the grade. Wind moved through the trusses, threading a low metallic hum through the structure.

Halfway across, the water opened beneath him.

The channel widened toward the bay, small boats idling near the far edge, waiting for tide or clearance. The bridge's pivot mechanism sat in the center span—heavy housing, greased and functional. When marine traffic required it, the entire roadway rotated, separating land from land with deliberate force.

Today it remained closed.

Zeb drove forward.

The sound persisted—metal under rubber, repetition without variation. It was the last assertive noise of the mainland. A final mechanical insistence before absorption. At the far end, the structure transitioned to asphalt with a muted shift. The percussive rhythm ended. The tires met smooth surface.

Silence did not arrive suddenly. It accumulated.

A small guard house stood on the island side, white paint sun-faded but intact. A man sat inside behind glass, not checking papers, not enforcing entry—simply marking passage. The window slid open as Zeb slowed.

"Afternoon, sir," the man said.

Zeb nodded once.

The barrier arm lifted with a slow mechanical hum.

The road narrowed further as it curved inland. Vegetation rose closer to the edges. Houses were not visible immediately. The island did not display itself at entry; it required progression.

He noticed, almost idly, that his body did not prepare.

No tightening at the shoulders. No anticipatory breath as the curve revealed more of the interior. The crossing had not triggered return in him. It had registered as sequence.

Behind him, the bridge remained visible for a few seconds through the rearview mirror—steel framework narrowing with distance, then disappearing behind tree line.

The island absorbed sound differently.

No traffic carried through. No distant engines layered the air. Wind moved through planted grasses and low palms designed to bend without noise. Even the birds held a different register—shorter calls, less sustained.

The house revealed itself where it always did—after the second bend, when the trees fell back just enough to permit alignment. White walls. Broad windows. Clean geometry mistaken for elegance.

Zeb turned into the drive and parked.

The engine cut. He stepped out.

The air carried salt and something recently cleaned. The island held sound differently—no engines idling, no distant traffic. Only wind moving through planted grasses and the faint, constant line of water beyond the dunes.

He stood briefly, calibrating scale.

Nothing in him braced.

The door opened easily.

Inside, the house maintained its temperature and its quiet with equal discipline. Light entered through angled glass and settled where it had always settled—diffused to prevent glare, curated to suggest calm rather than enforce it. Surfaces reflected without distortion. Someone had been maintaining the place carefully. Nothing had drifted.

Zeb set his bag near the entry and removed his jacket, folding it once before placing it over the back of a chair. The motion was automatic. His hands remembered placement without requiring emotional orientation.

A sound came from deeper inside—drawers closing, deliberate but unhurried.

Vivienne entered without announcement.

She wore linen, sleeves rolled once at the wrist, hair pulled back. She looked as she always did when moving through the house—composed not as performance, but as baseline. As if her day had begun before his arrival and would continue afterward without recalibration.

They stopped several feet apart. Neither advanced.

"You're here," she said.

"Yes," Zeb replied.

The exchange completed itself. Present-tense information. No inquiry folded into it.

She gestured lightly toward the counter. "I didn't realize you'd be coming through today."

"I didn't either."

The sentence landed without implication.

She studied him briefly—not searching, not measuring. Simply registering presence as one registers a change in weather that does not require adaptation.

"I have a call in a few minutes," she said. "From the mainland."

"Take it."

There was no generosity in the phrasing. No withdrawal either. It was logistical.

She nodded once and moved toward the far room. Her steps remained soft against the floor. Zeb did not follow her with his eyes. He did not convert her movement into meaning.

When he was alone again, the house remained unchanged.

That registered. Not as disappointment. Not as relief. As confirmation.

The structure did not respond to him. It did not activate memory or project expectation. It held its parameters.

Zeb walked toward the glass facing the water and looked out.

The sea moved steadily, indifferent to property lines. The tide did not adjust to architecture. The horizon remained level, unconcerned with ownership.

He watched for a moment, then turned away.

He had arrived.

Nothing shifted.

That was enough.

He picked up his jacket and moved deeper into the house—not to revisit it, but because the next room was where his bag needed to be.

The House as Object

The house revealed itself gradually, not because of size but because of design. It unfolded through corridors and controlled transitions, each threshold shaped to modulate experience without announcing that modulation.

Zeb moved through it at a natural pace, allowing walls and clearances to determine rhythm rather than memory. The floor plan remained intact. Lines held. Sightlines landed exactly where they were meant to.

The white had been refreshed—slightly warmer than before, perhaps to soften afternoon light. The shift was technical, not expressive. Maintenance, not reinvention.

Furniture occupied assigned geometries. Nothing crowded. Nothing drifted. A long table remained centered beneath a fixture scaled exactly to its proportions. Chairs were spaced evenly, correcting posture without demanding attention. Surfaces remained clear—objects reduced to function and accent. No accumulation. No entropy.

The precision registered cleanly.

It did not solicit agreement.

Windows opened onto the water at measured intervals. Not panoramic—curated. Each frame offered a portion of the sea that could be absorbed without overwhelming the eye. Light entered obliquely, settled across stone and wood, and thinned toward the ceiling.

The effect remained controlled calm.

The house resolved more quickly now—not because it had changed, but because he had.

Rooms that had once felt expansive now completed themselves without delay. Distances shortened perceptually. Transitions required no adjustment. What had once registered as atmosphere now resolved as layout.

Zeb did not compare this to before. The perception did not require contrast. It was simply how the structure presented itself to him now.

He paused near the center of the main room, not because anything called for attention, but because his body had finished orienting. He stood the way one stands in a lobby waiting for direction—present, uninvested, unopposed.

The house was neither persuasive nor inert.

It was exact.

He walked down the hall toward the bedroom.

The door stood open. The bed was made with the same squared corners, fabric pulled tight without strain. The room held its temperature evenly. Air moved quietly through vents designed not to announce themselves.

He stepped inside briefly, registered proportions, then stepped back out.

A bathroom door stood ajar. Fixtures gleamed. Towels were folded to consistent margins. The soap had been replaced with a newer version—same scent, different packaging. Continuity maintained through substitution.

Zeb did not touch anything.

It did not feel like restraint. It just felt unnecessary.

Memory did not activate in response to surfaces. No scenes replayed. No emotional residue clung to corners or thresholds. The house did not function as archive. It held no narrative leverage.

He passed the staircase without ascending. Upstairs did not require confirmation. The structure did not depend on inspection to remain intact.

In the far room, light pooled across the floor near the glass. Outside, the water moved steadily, unconcerned with alignment. The tide did not acknowledge architecture. That fact felt clean.

Zeb stood near the window and let his gaze move outward without holding it there.

The beauty remained.

It no longer organized him.

There was no desire to correct the house, reinterpret it, reclaim it, or reject it. He did not feel diminished by its order. He did not feel elevated by its restraint. The structure existed within its own precision.

The house had not changed.

His orientation had shifted.

He adjusted the sleeve of his shirt, smoothing the fabric once before letting his hand fall back to his side. The gesture was practical, unconscious.

He moved toward the next room because it was there.

Behind him, the house continued exactly as it had been designed to continue—beautiful, precise, and no longer instructive.

It did not ask anything of him.

And for the first time, that felt proportional.

Vivienne

Zeb encountered Vivienne again without ceremony.

She entered as he was rinsing a glass at the sink, sleeves still rolled, hair secured at the back of her neck with the same practical restraint he had noticed earlier. The motion of her arrival did not alter the room. She adjusted her path slightly to move around him, the choreography of shared space long internalized.

"I'll be out for a while," she said, setting her phone beside a folder on the counter. "Dinner at the club."

"Okay," Zeb replied.

The exchange completed itself.

She crossed to the cabinet without pause. Drawers opened without resistance. A hinge closed softly. The house responded to her presence the way it always had—not with warmth, not with emphasis, but with correct calibration. Her movements did not disturb the space. They aligned with it.

Zeb dried the glass and set it upside down on the rack. He did not watch her. He did not avoid watching her. His attention remained with the task until it was complete, then shifted without hesitation.

Vivienne opened the folder, scanned a page, then slid it back into place. The gesture suggested organization rather than urgency. Her posture held no tension. If anything, it carried the steadiness of someone accustomed to small systems operating correctly.

"They're changing the dock schedule next week," she said. "Service hours are shifting earlier."

"Good to know."

He did not ask who had decided. He did not ask why. The information arrived without demand.

She nodded once, satisfied that the fact had been transferred, and leaned lightly against the counter. The distance between them remained unnegotiated—neither close nor staged as apart.

For a moment, neither spoke.

The silence did not gather weight. It existed because nothing required filling. The house held it easily.

"You're only here briefly?" she asked.

"Yes."

He did not attach duration. Did not soften the statement. Did not frame it as apology or explanation.

She studied him for a second—not probing, not evaluating. Simply registering scale.

"All right," she said.

The word carried no adjustment. No attempt to reposition herself inside his stay. No negotiation of proximity.

Zeb noticed, neutrally, that he did not feel the reflex to clarify. No impulse to say how long. No instinct to offer the outline of a return. The answer had been sufficient. It did not need reinforcement.

Vivienne checked her watch and slipped the folder into her bag. The movement was economical. She had always been precise about transitions—never abrupt, never hesitant. Completion without ceremony.

"They'll probably be late," she said. "They usually are."

A faint smile appeared—less about humor than about pattern recognition.

"Mm," Zeb said.

She remained leaning against the counter for a moment longer. Not waiting. Not lingering. The pause felt like a system idling before shifting gears.

Zeb became aware—not as discomfort, not as longing—that there had once been a different version of this pause. One in which one of them would have filled it. A question about the guest list. A remark about who would attend. A shared prediction about how the evening would unfold.

That version did not present itself.

The absence did not bruise.

It simply registered as obsolete.

Vivienne straightened and moved toward the door, one hand resting briefly on the frame.

"You can use the car if you need it," she said.

"I won't need it."

She nodded once. The offer had been procedural. Its refusal remained the same.

For a fraction of a second, Zeb sensed the possibility of an additional sentence. Not heavy. Not overdue. Something minor—an adjustment to tone, perhaps. A small connective thread.

It did not arrive.

She adjusted the strap of her bag and stepped out onto the path. The door closed behind her with its usual soft restraint.

Zeb remained at the counter.

He noticed that he did not listen for the cadence of her footsteps diminishing along the path. He did not track whether she turned left or right. He did not picture the clubhouse, the dock lights, the polished bar, the conversations that would layer themselves across the evening.

That reflex—once automatic—did not activate.

The absence felt clean. Not detachment. Not correction.

More like jurisdiction returning to its appropriate boundary.

He rinsed his hands and dried them, though they were not wet enough to require it. The gesture was habitual, not symbolic.

He moved toward the window.

Outside, the path curved gently away from the house, bordered by low grasses designed to bend without breaking. The geometry of resilience was consistent throughout the island. Structures yielded without appearing to do so.

Farther out, the water held its steady line against the horizon.

Zeb watched until a boat he had noticed earlier slipped behind a stand of trees.

The encounter did not replay.

There was no line he wished to revise. No tonal adjustment to consider. No calculation of what might have been implied or withheld.

The interaction had occurred.

It had ended.

Nothing remained suspended between them.

He turned back into the house, not marking her departure, not following it internally—simply continuing along the line of his own attention.

The imbalance remained.

But it no longer suggested correction.

It existed as structure.

And like everything else in the house, it settled into function.

Memory Without Adhesion

Zeb moved through the house without direction. Not searching. Not avoiding. Simply crossing rooms because they were there.

The hallway enforced a single line of movement. Pale wood underfoot, grain running lengthwise as if encouraging forward motion. The walls had been repainted since he was last there—same color, newer finish. The light from the far window reached only partway down the corridor, stopping where it always had, thinning before it reached the turn.

He paused once near the threshold of the bedroom. Not intentionally. Just enough to register scale.

The air held a faint, layered smell—cleaning solution over salt, and beneath it something floral, residual, diluted. He could not name it. He did not try to. Recognition arrived without emotional instruction.

Images surfaced. Not in sequence. Not with narrative edges.

A shirt folded at the foot of the bed. Her voice from the bathroom, indistinct through water and tile. The sound of running water extending longer than necessary. Late afternoon light pooling on the floor while the rest of the room remained dim.

The images did not assemble. They appeared the way reflections do on glass when the angle is wrong—present, partial, already dissolving before they could stabilize.

Zeb waited, briefly, for the feeling that once followed such recall.

It did not arrive.

No tightening in the chest. No subtle draw inward. No instinct to convert the fragments into regret, gratitude, accusation, or meaning.

The images hovered, then thinned.

He stepped fully into the room. The furniture had been adjusted. The bed lower than he remembered. The nightstand replaced with something simpler, less ornamental. A book lay face down near the lamp, its spine uncreased, a thin line marking where it had been left open.

He registered the changes as information.

Another memory surfaced—not visual at first, but postural.

Standing here once, jacket still on. Listening to her speak from behind him. The weight settling onto one leg as he waited for something—agreement, perhaps. Or conclusion.

The words themselves did not return. Only the stance—the sensation of being positioned inside a conversation he believed would define something.

That memory, too, stalled. It did not open into explanation. It did not produce correction. It ended at the edge of posture.

Zeb crossed to the window.

The view was unchanged. Water extending outward in an uninterrupted line. The horizon steady and unresponsive. The late light flattened contrast, reducing depth to gradation.

The glass reflected part of the room back at him, faintly.

Another fragment surfaced.

Standing here at night. Lights off behind him. The room invisible in the glass. Her reflection faint beside his, the two shapes nearly indistinguishable in the dark. The sense—then—that the moment was holding something fragile, something that could be secured if handled correctly.

The fragility did not return.

What remained was geometry.

Two figures in a pane of glass. Light behind them. Nothing more.

He did not feel relief at the absence.

He noticed it the way one notices a sound stopping—a fan switched off in another room. The quiet afterward was not triumphant. It simply occupied space that had been filled.

Zeb turned away.

The bathroom door stood open. The mirror above the sink caught the light without distortion.

He glanced at it.

Another image: steam once fogging that glass. His hand tracing a circle through condensation. The partial face that had appeared inside it—distorted, playful, then serious. The weight he had assigned to that moment at the time. The conviction that shared smallness meant permanence.

Now, the image held no authority.

It did not argue for reinstatement. It did not petition for reinterpretation. It was simply something that had occurred.

Zeb washed his hands. The water ran clear and unremarkable. He dried them and turned off the light.

As he moved back toward the main room, he noticed the silence again—not as presence, but as absence of pressure. The house did not amplify recollection. It did not echo it back at him.

Memory continued to surface, sporadically.

A laugh from the far end of the hall. The clink of ice against glass. The weight of the couch beneath him as he leaned forward, elbows on knees, listening intently to something that once seemed consequential.

Each fragment arrived intact and left untouched.

There was no adhesive.

He did not analyze the absence. He did not label it healing. He did not call it detachment. He did not translate it into growth.

He simply observed that the memories no longer organized his interior movement.

They did not point forward. They did not pull backward. Nor did they rearrange his posture inside a room.

They had become inert.

This surprised him—not sharply, but steadily.

Not because he wanted them to matter. But because they had mattered for so long.

He had assumed, without interrogating the assumption, that their gravity would persist.

He stood near the doorway that led toward the path and the water. Light from outside reached inward in a narrow band, stopping just short of his shoes.

Another memory began to form—standing in this exact place once, hesitating before leaving. Believing that hesitation itself was meaningful. Believing that delay equaled depth.

The belief did not reconstruct.

The memory stalled before it could gather force.

Zeb stepped forward, crossing the threshold.

Behind him, the house remained as it was.

The memories did not follow.

They had lost jurisdiction.

The World Continues

Zeb's phone vibrated once in his pocket. Not insistently. Not with urgency.

Just enough to register.

The sound was muted by fabric, more pressure than tone. A brief reminder that something elsewhere had advanced by a degree.

He stopped near the path that led away from the house, where sand thinned into packed earth and low grasses bordered the walkway. The trees opened slightly toward the water there, creating a narrow view of the bay through layered green.

He did not check the screen immediately.

The vibration did not carry consequence until it was acknowledged.

For a few seconds, it remained suspended—information unclaimed.

When he did look, it was a message from work.

A detail. A timing correction. A confirmation that something had shifted forward by a few hours and would need minor adjustment.

Nothing more.

Zeb read it once, then again more slowly. The language was precise but not alarmed. No cascading implication. No urgency disguised as courtesy.

He typed a brief response—accurate, unadorned. A confirmation of receipt. A small recalibration. No explanation attached. No context offered beyond what was necessary.

He closed the thread.

The exchange took less than a minute.

When it ended, there was no feeling of interruption.

The house behind him did not recede dramatically. It did not ask to be re-evaluated in light of the message. It remained where it was—white lines, glass, contained light—unconcerned with schedules.

Zeb slid the phone back into his pocket.

Wind moved through the trees in uneven currents. The sound did not repeat exactly. Leaves shifted against one another in soft friction. Somewhere inland, a low mechanical hum continued—a generator or a maintenance vehicle idling out of sight.

The soft, irregular rhythm of water reached him in fragments, filtered by distance and dune.

Laughter carried briefly from the direction of the club house. It arrived in partial syllables, detached from context. Another voice answered, lower, indistinct. The sound thinned before it reached the path.

The present did not assert itself forcefully.

It simply continued.

Zeb noticed that he did not feel disloyal to what had happened inside the house.

There was no internal defense required. No justification assembled. No hierarchy of importance to negotiate.

The past did not compete. It did not request preservation. It had ceased to petition.

He adjusted the strap of his bag on his shoulder and continued down the path.

His pace remained unchanged.

He did not accelerate to match the message. He did not slow to prolong the quiet.

The world did not require him to choose between them.

Halfway down the path, he encountered a slight fork—one direction leading toward the dock and marina, the other curving inland toward the club house and parking area.

He paused only long enough to let someone pass.

A man walked by carrying a crate of bottled water balanced against his hip, headed toward the club house. He nodded once, casual and procedural. Zeb returned the nod.

No recognition followed. The man did not look back.

Zeb resumed walking toward the dock.

Another vibration.

This one shorter. Less layered.

A logistics update unrelated to the first. A confirmation that someone else had already adjusted the timeline.

Zeb read it. Replied with a single line. Closed it.

The system had absorbed the change.

He put the phone away again.

The dock extended outward in clean lines, boards bleached by sun and repaired in sections where necessary. Boats shifted slightly in their slips, restrained by lines that allowed motion without release.

Engines started and stopped without ceremony. A man further down the pier tightened a rope and stepped back to assess the angle.

Nothing in the scene required attention beyond what it already had.

Zeb did not stop to look back at the house.

He did not feel compelled to confirm its position in the landscape.

The water moved steadily beyond the marina, surface broken by small wakes that dissolved quickly.

The bridge remained somewhere behind the tree line, out of view, rotating when required.

The house remained where it had been.

The messages continued to arrive at intervals that did not concern the island.

Zeb adjusted to each without friction.

He did not feel restored.

He did not feel diminished.

He felt aligned.

The world continued.

He moved within it.

Indifference Clarified

Morning arrived without emphasis.

Light entered the room evenly, flattening the edges of furniture before settling into place. The house did not feel altered by the night. It held its temperature. Its proportions.

Vivienne had already left.

He knew this not because he heard her go, but because the absence carried no delay. The kitchen had been reset. A cup rinsed and inverted beside the sink. The air faintly marked by coffee that had already dissipated.

There was no note.

There did not need to be.

Zeb stood for a moment near the window, allowing the previous evening to surface.

Dinner had proceeded as expected.

The club's dining room had been softly lit, tables arranged to preserve distance rather than intimacy. The conversation had moved in low currents between them—business, travel, small recalibrations of status.

They had walked back along the path afterward, neither accelerating nor slowing. The night air had been cooler than earlier in the day. She had mentioned a schedule adjustment for the following week. He had nodded.

Nothing had sharpened.

Nothing had frayed.

Back inside, they had moved through the house in parallel lines. Doors opened. Water ran briefly. Lights extinguished one by one.

If she had expected a conversation beyond sequence, she had not signaled it.

He had slept without interruption.

The memory of the evening did not expand.

It settled into place as one more completed movement—accurate, intact, inert.

Zeb turned away from the window.

He packed without haste.

The room he had been using was spare—temporary by design. A bed, a table, a chair. Nothing arranged to be remembered. Nothing layered with accumulation.

He folded his clothes methodically. Not in the tightened efficiency he once associated with leaving. There was no urgency to outpace, no atmosphere to exit before it shifted. Each item returned to its place without negotiation.

He noticed, distantly, that nothing in him resisted the act.

There was no tightening as the bag filled. No reflexive inventory of what might be left behind. No internal calculation of what the departure meant.

Packing did not register as closure.

It registered as sequence.

He paused once, holding a shirt he had worn to dinner the night before. The fabric carried no residue beyond ordinary use. He waited to see whether anything would attach itself—an inflection in her voice, a gesture across the table, a look he might have once interpreted as signal.

Nothing did.

The absence felt stable.

He folded the shirt and placed it in the bag.

There was nothing in the room that required leaving behind. No object that asked to remain. No gesture that needed staging.

He moved through the space once more, confirming completion rather than revisiting. The floor clear. The table empty. The chair aligned. The window closed.

There was nothing to schedule.

Outside, the island had resumed its ordinary rhythm. Service carts moved along the drive. A groundskeeper adjusted a line of irrigation. The air held the low salt of morning.

Zeb stepped onto the path without looking back at the house.

It remained where it had been.

He did not consider whether Vivienne would return before he left. He did not rehearse explanation. The previous evening had concluded without tension; it required no extension.

As he passed the club house, a staff member unlocked the side door and propped it open. Someone inside was already arranging tables for the next meal. The room that had held them hours earlier showed no trace of occupation.

He did not feel erased.

He felt correctly scaled.

The past had narrowed to what it was: something that had occurred.

Nothing here required continuation.

At the edge of the drive, he placed his bag in the back of the vehicle and closed the latch. The sound registered cleanly. Not heavy. Not symbolic.

Finished.

He entered the driver's seat and turned the key.

The island did not register his leaving.

It resumed.

Orientation Forward

The bridge received him without adjustment.

The tires met steel. The familiar hollow rhythm rose through the chassis, steady and unvaried. The truss structure held its shape against the sky, rivets darkened by weather but intact.

Halfway across, water widened beneath him. A boat moved slowly along the channel, wake dissolving behind it. The pivot mechanism at the center span remained locked in place.

The crossing did not announce itself.

It functioned.

Zeb drove on.

Metal gave way to asphalt with a muted shift. The percussive pattern dissolved into the layered hum of mainland traffic. Signals changed. Cars merged. The sound field thickened.

Nothing followed him across.

He did not inventory what had been left.

There was nothing pending.

Solitude arrived without emphasis.

Earlier in his life, it would have demanded accounting—what had been lost, what had ended, what required correction. Now it arrived neutrally, like a change in weather that did not require preparation.

Clarity no longer required departure for him.

His attention remained continuous—neither sharpened nor diffused.

He drove on.

He drove without adjusting pace. No part of him remained oriented backward. The island had returned to geography.

Traffic thickened as he neared the mainland proper. Signals shifted. Lanes narrowed and widened again. The sound field layered itself gradually—engines, brakes, distant construction, a radio from the car beside him pulsing faintly through closed windows.

Nothing in him resisted the reintegration.

He stopped once for fuel. Once for coffee. The transactions were brief, unremarkable. A receipt printed. A card returned. A nod exchanged with a clerk who did not look up.

The day unfolded in segments rather than events.

A call from work. A recalibration of timing. Two short emails sent from the parking lot outside a warehouse he had no reason to enter.

No urgency. No backlog demanding interpretation.

By afternoon he was back in the city proper, the air carrying a different density—less salt, more exhaust and stone. He did not accelerate to compensate. He did not slow to extend anything.

Time passed without resistance.

When evening came, it did so gradually. Light thinned between buildings. Windows along the street shifted from reflective to luminous. Pedestrians thickened, then dispersed again.

At the place he was staying, he parked and carried his bag inside.

The room accepted him without response.

He set the bag down where it belonged—not precisely, just correctly. The weight left his shoulder and did not echo.

He unpacked what was necessary. The rest remained folded, available, unpressing.

There was no impulse to reorganize the space. No adjustment required to make it habitable. It already was.

He washed his hands. The water ran clear. He dried them and stood for a moment at the sink, not reflecting, simply still long enough for the day to settle into its completed shape.

He turned off the overhead light, leaving one lamp on near the wall.

The light settled evenly across the room.

Nothing shifted.

Outside, a car door closed. Footsteps passed in the hall. Somewhere, a phone vibrated and stopped. A television murmured briefly through the wall and then went silent.

He did not check his phone.

There was nothing waiting.

He reached out and switched the lamp off.

The room went dark.

It did not feel like an ending.

It felt like sequence.

Outside, traffic continued at intervals. An elevator door opened and closed somewhere below. The city held its own rhythm without reference to him.

The world held.

He moved within it.

CHAPTER 17

A Life Built, Not Displayed

The morning did not announce itself. Zeb woke before the alarm—not from need, but because his body had settled into the rhythm of the place. Light filtered in at an angle that suggested time without insisting on it. The room was quiet without asking to be noticed.

He lay still for a moment. Breath came evenly. The day arrived not as possibility or burden, but as sequence.

He got up.

The floor was cool beneath his feet. He crossed the room and opened the window a few inches, enough to let the air move through without changing the temperature. Outside, ordinary sounds registered—distant traffic, someone moving a cart, a voice carrying briefly and then dissolving.

In the kitchen, the light above the sink flickered once before settling. He made coffee the same way he always did—without ceremony. Water measured by habit. Grounds leveled with the back of the spoon. The kettle's low sound building, then cutting cleanly when it reached the right pitch.

He did not think about whether anyone else was awake.

When she entered a few minutes later, it was without announcement. No greeting. No smile meant to mark the start of the day. She crossed to the counter, reached for a cup, and waited while the coffee finished.

"Did you sleep?" she asked, not turning.

"Yes," he said.

She nodded. That was enough.

They moved around each other without choreography. When she reached for the cabinet, he stepped aside. When he opened the drawer beneath the counter, she shifted her weight without comment. Their movements overlapped cleanly, without apology or signal.

They stood together for a few moments drinking coffee. Not facing one another. Not sharing a view. Just occupying the same space while the morning continued to assemble itself.

Outside, a truck passed. Somewhere nearby, metal struck concrete and then stopped. A door opened and closed. The day did not adjust to them.

She rinsed her cup and set it in the rack. Zeb finished his and did the same. The rack was already half full from the night before. Neither of them rearranged it. It would dry as it dried.

"I'll take care of the forms later," she said, pulling on a jacket.

"Okay," Zeb said. "I'll be back before noon."

There was no discussion beyond that. The information wasn't reassurance. It simply placed the day into motion.

He picked up the bag he used for work—not heavy, not empty. Papers inside, a notebook, nothing he needed to protect. He checked the contents once, not to make sure anything was there, but to make sure nothing unnecessary was.

At the door, he paused briefly—not to say anything, not to register separation. Just long enough to put his shoes on evenly.

She was already moving toward the table, sorting through a stack of mail. She glanced up once.

"Keys," she said.

He reached into the bowl by the door and slid them across to her. She caught them without looking.

Zeb opened the door and stepped outside.

The air carried the faint smell of salt and heat. The street was already active—not busy, just underway. He walked at a pace that matched no one else's and did not require adjustment.

As he moved away from the house, nothing in him tried to register it.

This was not peace. It was baseline.

Later, when he stopped briefly at a corner to let a group pass, he noticed his body didn't argue with the day.

Nothing in him was being proved. Nothing in him was being withheld.

The day opened in front of him without invitation or resistance, and he stepped into it the way one steps into a task that has already begun.

Shared Labor

The work did not begin together.

Zeb was already at the table when she came in, papers spread in a loose stack, not arranged for clarity so much as access. He was making notes in the margin of one page, crossing out a line on another, moving between them without sequence. The room held the low noise of ordinary activity—water running somewhere nearby, a fan turning, the faint sound of her typing at the counter.

She moved through the space without announcing herself. Set a bag down. Opened a drawer. Closed it again. The sounds layered without interrupting one another.

Zeb reached for a different pen when the first ran dry. He did not look up.

She began preparing food—not a meal exactly, more like readiness. Vegetables rinsed and set aside. A pan placed on the stove and left cold for the moment. Something pulled from the refrigerator and returned when it was clear it would not be needed yet.

There was no conversation about sequence.

At some point, she moved the stack of mail that had been sitting at the edge of the table for days, sorted it quickly, and slid two envelopes toward Zeb without comment. He glanced at them, nodded once, and placed them beneath the papers he was already working through.

Neither explained the gesture.

Zeb stood to refill his coffee and paused when he realized the kettle was already warm. She had turned it on earlier without saying so. He poured, set the kettle back in place, and left the cup on the counter rather than bringing it back to the table. He would drink it later.

She wiped her hands on a towel and picked up a notebook, flipping through a few pages until she found what she was looking for. The page was half full already—lists, dates, a few items crossed out. She added one more line and closed it.

They moved around each other easily. When she opened the cabinet beneath the sink, he shifted his chair back without thinking.

When he reached for the printer on the side table, she stepped aside, continuing what she was doing without pause.

Their proximity was practical.

At one point, a pan heated too quickly and she turned the knob down without looking. Zeb noticed only because the sound changed. He did not comment. He made a note on the page in front of him and continued.

He registered, distantly, that this would once have unsettled him—shared space, work unfolding without signal.

Now it didn't.

He felt neither watched nor responsible for managing tone or pace. He did not wonder whether he was doing enough, or whether what he was doing would be noticed. The absence of evaluation allowed the work to proceed cleanly.

She crossed the room carrying a small stack of containers and placed them on the counter beside the sink. Zeb glanced up long enough to see that they were empty, then returned to his notes. A moment later, she asked, "Did you want these labeled?"

"Yes," he said. "Just dates."

She nodded and picked up a marker.

No further instruction was required.

The fan clicked off automatically when the room cooled. Neither of them noticed until the sound was gone. The quiet that followed was not marked.

Zeb finished with one set of papers and slid them into a folder. He set the folder at the edge of the table, where it would be seen when it needed to be. He did not announce that he was done. She did not ask.

She began cleaning the counter, moving items aside as needed, returning them once the surface was clear. When she reached the space where Zeb's coffee cup sat, she moved it slightly to the left and wiped beneath it. Zeb noticed and did not react. He would drink from it later.

At some point, he stood and joined her at the counter, not to help, just because the next thing he needed was there. He rinsed his hands, dried them, and reached for the containers she had labeled. He stacked them neatly and placed them in the bag by the door.

She watched him do this only long enough to confirm it was done.

They worked like this for a while—tasks beginning and ending without ceremony, responsibilities passing between them without exchange. No one thanked anyone. No one checked in.

Zeb noticed his body stayed settled. The work stayed the work. He did not wonder if this was love, or partnership, or something else that required a name.

It was simply reliable.

When the timer on the stove sounded, she turned it off and moved the pan aside. Zeb continued sorting papers. The smell of food registered and then faded into the background.

Eventually, she picked up her bag and checked the time. "I'm heading out," she said.

"Okay," Zeb replied.

She left the room without pause.

Zeb remained at the table, finishing what he was doing. The work did not change shape in her absence. He closed the last folder, stacked it with the others, and stood.

The room continued. He stood and moved on.

Decisions Without Explanation

On another morning, they left at the same time.

Zeb registered it only once they were already at the door—he tightening the strap on his bag, she glancing at her phone and slipping it into her pocket without comment.

Outside, the weather had shifted slightly. The light was flatter than it had been earlier. Heat lingered but no longer pressed.

She picked up her keys.

Zeb reached for his jacket.

They stepped outside without clarifying destination.

They stepped outside together and turned in the same direction without looking at one another. The choice did not feel shared so much as aligned. No pause occurred where preference might surface. No moment opened for negotiation.

They walked.

A few blocks in, they passed the corner where they would usually split. Zeb noticed it in the same way he noticed his breathing—present, but not directive. He did not slow. She did not angle away. They continued straight.

The street narrowed slightly ahead. Construction had redirected foot traffic, pushing people closer together without forcing interaction. Zeb adjusted his pace to accommodate the change without thinking. She did the same, a half step later, not mirroring— just responding to the same conditions.

They reached a small market near the water. The door was open; the air was cooler. She stepped in. Zeb followed.

No one suggested it. No one checked for agreement. The decision did not register as concession or initiative. It simply occurred.

Inside, the shelves were half stocked. A delivery was in progress, boxes stacked near the back. Zeb picked up two items without comparing prices or options and set them on the counter. She added one more and moved aside to let someone pass.

At the register, the clerk spoke quickly and without interest. Zeb paid. She took the bag and carried it out.

Outside again, the light had shifted further. They walked toward the water, then turned onto a quieter street without comment. The bag changed hands once when her grip loosened. Zeb took it without acknowledgment and carried it the rest of the way.

They stopped near a low wall where others sometimes sat, though no one was there now. Zeb set the bag down and took out what they had bought. There was no arrangement, no division. Each of them ate what was nearest.

Zeb noticed that he did not feel the need to assert preference—no impulse to claim the better portion, no calculation about fairness. He also did not feel the familiar vigilance that came with shared choice, the quiet fear of being overridden or subsumed.

The structure held without pressure.

They ate, not talking. When the food was gone, the bag folded itself into nothing and was set aside. Zeb checked his watch once, not to measure the moment, just to confirm the next interval.

"I should head back," she said, eventually.

Zeb nodded. "I've got a call."

They stood.

There was no reference to what they had done or why. No sense that the decision required memory or reinforcement. It had already dissolved into the afternoon.

They separated at the next intersection, each turning away without marking it. Zeb continued on, the path opening ahead of him in its usual way.

Later, when he tried to recall what they had eaten—or why they'd gone that way—nothing distinct surfaced. The choice hadn't lodged as event or symbol.

It had simply allowed the day to proceed.

And the day kept moving.

Work Continues

The work resumed.

Zeb sat at the table with his laptop open, a legal pad beside it, phone face down within reach. The room held the late-morning light evenly, neither bright nor dim. Outside, someone passed with a cart. The sound registered and moved on.

He read through a document once without marking it. The second time, he made two notes in the margin and closed the file. Nothing required extended deliberation. The problems were familiar, the constraints clear.

He dialed into a call at the scheduled time.

Voices joined one by one. Names were exchanged quickly, then dropped. The conversation moved where it needed to go—deadlines, scope, a correction to something that had been assumed incorrectly earlier in the week. Zeb listened more than he spoke. When he did speak, it was to narrow the question, not expand it.

He did not perform authority. He did not defer.

The work held.

Across the room, the woman moved in and out of the space intermittently. At one point she sat near the window, sorting through her own materials. At another, she stepped outside briefly and returned. Her presence did not register as distraction or anchor. It was simply part of the environment—like the light, like the air.

Zeb noticed that his attention did not fracture.

In the past, work and intimacy had existed in competition—one demanding exclusion of the other. Focus had required withdrawal. Presence had required absence elsewhere. Now, neither asked for that.

He ended the call when the agenda was complete. No one lingered. No unnecessary follow-up surfaced. He noted one action item and set it aside for later.

He wrote for a while after that.

The writing was direct. Functional. He did not search for the right phrasing beyond clarity. Each paragraph ended where it should. When a sentence did not belong, he removed it without hesitation.

The woman crossed behind him once, reaching for something on the counter. Zeb shifted his chair slightly to make room. The adjustment was physical, not symbolic. He returned to his work immediately.

He noticed, distantly, that there was no sense of divided life.

Nothing in him was pulled toward the other room as if something more important were happening there. Nothing in him resisted the work as intrusion. The domains did not compete. They coexisted without hierarchy.

At some point, his phone buzzed with a message. He glanced at it, responded with a single line, and placed the phone back where it had been. The interruption did not linger.

He finished the section he was working on and closed the document. The task was complete—not because time had run out, not because something else demanded precedence, but because it had reached its natural end.

He stood and stretched his shoulders once.

The woman looked up briefly from where she was sitting.

"I'm heading out for a bit," she said.

"Okay," Zeb replied.

She left the room. The sound of the door closing was unremarkable.

Zeb remained at the table for another few minutes, reviewing his notes and placing them into a folder. He shut the laptop and slid it into his bag. The work did not cling to him. It stayed where it belonged.

When he stood, it was without transition.

The day continued.

Time Passing Without Accounting

The days did not separate themselves.

They arrived with small variations—light shifting slightly earlier or later, the air warmer one afternoon than the next—but nothing announced itself as change. Zeb noticed these differences only in passing, the way one notices weather without assigning it narrative.

Morning routines repeated without exactness. Coffee brewed. Papers gathered. Messages checked and answered. Sometimes she left first. Sometimes he did. Sometimes they crossed paths in the doorway and adjusted without comment.

Meals happened when they happened.

Occasionally they ate together at the table. Other times one of them arrived while the other was already finishing. There was no effort to synchronize. Food was prepared, eaten, cleared. The kitchen returned to its neutral state without insistence.

Work continued.

Zeb took calls at different hours. Some days he wrote more than he spoke. Other days he spoke almost continuously and wrote very little. He noticed that his energy did not spike or drain dramatically. It held.

The woman moved through her own schedule nearby— sometimes present, sometimes not. Her absence did not register as lack. Her presence did not register as event.

They did not recount their days to one another.

Information passed when it needed to—where someone would be later, whether something had been handled, if a delivery was expected. Nothing was framed as sharing. It was logistical, sufficient.

At night, the house settled in the same way each time. Lights went off room by room. Doors closed or stayed open based on temperature rather than symbolism. Zeb slept deeply more often than not.

He woke without anticipation or dread.

Time moved forward without bargaining.

Once, he noticed that a meeting he would normally have left early for had been rescheduled. He adjusted his day without commentary. Another time, she changed plans in the afternoon and returned later than expected. Zeb registered the difference only when she came through the door.

Neither explained.

The continuity did not require reinforcement.

Zeb realized, without pausing on the thought, that nothing was being stored against the future. No credit accumulated. No effort banked. The days did not feel like investment or rehearsal.

Stability did not present itself as something fragile.

It did not feel as though it could be broken by inattention.

One evening, Zeb found himself alone in the house for an hour or two. The light outside faded gradually. He turned on a lamp when it grew dim enough to require it. He read a few pages of a book and set it down without finishing the chapter.

The quiet did not press.

It did not ask to be filled or explained.

When the door opened later and she returned, Zeb did not mark the transition. He looked up briefly, nodded, and returned to what he had been doing.

The day continued as if it had never needed confirmation.

And when, later still, Zeb stood alone again at the window for a moment—watching the street below move at its usual pace—he noticed that the solitude did not register as interruption.

It was simply another condition the day passed through.

Nothing had been counted. The time remained.

Presence *Without* Narration

The evening assembled without instruction.

Zeb was already in the kitchen, a pan warming slowly on the stove. He adjusted the heat once, then stepped back. She set a bag on the chair, washed her hands, and reached for the cutting board without speaking.

They worked side by side.

Vegetables were sliced and set aside. A pot was filled and placed on the back burner. A cabinet opened and closed. The sequence held without commentary. When Zeb reached across the counter for salt, she shifted the board slightly to clear space. Neither acknowledged the movement.

The pan hissed briefly and then settled.

They ate at the table when the food was ready. Plates were filled unevenly. Zeb took the chair nearest the wall. She sat opposite him, angled slightly away. No attempt was made to face each other fully.

Cutlery moved. Water was poured. The room held the small sounds of eating without interruption.

When Zeb finished, he stood and carried his plate to the sink. She remained seated, finishing her meal. He rinsed his plate and set it in the rack, then wiped the counter where a drop of water had landed.

She joined him a moment later and placed her plate beside his.

They did not speak.

Afterward, Zeb moved to the table with his laptop and opened it without urgency. She sat nearby with a book, reading a few pages at a time, pausing occasionally to mark her place with a finger before continuing.

The room remained in use.

A notification sounded once. Zeb glanced at the screen and dismissed it. He typed for a few minutes, stopped, read over what he had written, and closed the laptop. The task had reached its limit for the evening.

She turned a page.

Zeb stood and stretched his shoulders once, then crossed the room to turn off the overhead light. The lamp near the wall remained on, casting enough light to continue.

Neither commented on the change.

He returned to the table and sat again, resting his hands where the laptop had been. She shifted slightly in her chair to keep reading.

The evening continued.

Later, when the book closed and the lamp was turned off, the room settled into its final shape without pause. Zeb stood, rinsed his hands, and dried them. She gathered her things and placed them where they belonged.

They moved toward the hallway without coordination.

Nothing in the room signaled that something had occurred.

The night held, unadorned.

And the day passed into the next without needing to be named.

The Life, Unremarked

Zeb noticed the hinge before he noticed the door.

It caught slightly when he closed it—nothing broken, just a fraction of resistance where the metal met wood. The sound was small and unfinished, the kind that only registered if one was already paying attention.

He opened the door again and adjusted the screws a quarter turn with the tool from the sink drawer. The hinge settled. He closed the door. This time it held cleanly.

He didn't test it again.

The room was otherwise unchanged. The table held what it held. The chair was where it had been left. The light from the window thinned as the afternoon moved toward evening.

Zeb put the tool away.

He noticed there was no bracing. The steadiness that had been building over time remained unchallenged.

He moved through the space, picking up a book that had been left on the arm of the chair and returning it to the shelf. Not in its precise location—just where it belonged. He straightened the edge of a rug where it had folded slightly under the table leg and left it at that.

These actions felt like use.

The woman crossed the room behind him, carrying a stack of papers. She set them down on the counter and left again without comment. Zeb continued what he was doing without pause.

Outside, the day thinned further. A voice carried briefly through the open window and then disappeared. Somewhere nearby, something mechanical started and stopped.

Zeb checked the latch on the window and closed it partway when the air cooled. The sound of the city softened but did not disappear.

He stood there for a moment—not reflecting, not pausing for effect—simply long enough for the next task to arrive. When it did, he moved toward it without hesitation.

There was no sense of completion. No quiet triumph.

The life he was living did not announce itself.

Zeb turned off the light in the room and walked down the hallway, leaving the space exactly as it was meant to be used again. The door closed behind him.

222

CHAPTER 18

Water ran before he adjusted the temperature. He stood at the sink long enough for the chill to leave the pipes, then washed his hands without looking at the mirror above the basin. The light was thin and even, coming in from the side.

He dried his hands and returned the towel to its hook.

In the kitchen, the kettle was still warm from the night before. He filled it, set it on the burner, and turned the flame low. While it heated, he opened the cabinet and took down a mug—plain, unmarked, one of several identical ones. Coffee went into the filter. He did not measure. The water reached its point and clicked off. He poured it through slowly, watched it rise, then stepped away while it finished.

Outside, something moved—a door, a voice, footsteps crossing the path—but the room remained unchanged. He stood at the counter, waiting without checking the time.

When the coffee was ready, he poured it and took the first sip standing. It was hot enough to require attention, not enough to interrupt. He drank the rest more slowly, then rinsed the mug and set it in the rack to dry.

late morning

He opened the laptop and let it wake fully before touching anything. Messages loaded in their own time. He read the first without answering, then the second, then a third that required a response he did not yet have. He closed it.

A document waited where he had left it. He read from the top, corrected a sentence, removed a word that no longer belonged. The change shortened the paragraph. He continued until the file reached its end, then stopped without deciding whether it was finished.

He answered two messages quickly. Another he left open, cursor blinking at the start of a reply. He did not rush it. He did not return to it either.

A call came in. He took it standing, listening more than he spoke. When it ended, he wrote down a time and a name on a scrap of paper, folded it once, and set it beside the keyboard.

He read again, this time something unrelated. A few pages in, he marked a passage and closed the book.

One task ended. Another paused.

He stood, stretched once, and closed the laptop without checking what remained.

midday

He left the house with a list he did not look at again. At the market, he took what he needed from the shelf and set it on the counter without arranging it. The cashier rang it through, paused once to fix a number, then handed him the receipt.

"Have a good day," she said.

"You too," he answered, already stepping aside.

Outside, a man he recognized but did not know nodded once as they passed. Zeb returned it without breaking stride.

He crossed the square and stopped briefly when someone ahead of him did. When the path cleared, he continued.

By the time he reached the next corner, the exchange had already dissolved.

afternoon

He walked toward the center of the island along the paved path, stepping aside once to let a cart pass, then again near the clubhouse where people gathered and dispersed without pattern. He crossed the courtyard, followed the marked path along the trees, and turned where it narrowed.

At the dock, he waited until boarding began. He stood near the rail, shifted once to make space. When it docked on the far side, he stepped off with the others and walked two blocks inland.

He stopped once to check an address, adjusted his direction, and continued. One errand took longer than expected. Another required only a signature.

On the return trip, he boarded the earlier ferry instead of the later one. No one commented. He took the same place near the rail and stepped off when it reached the island.

He walked back the way he had come, turning where the path widened, then narrowing again toward the house.

late afternoon

He set the box on the table and opened it. Inside, the parts were already separated. He took one out, aligned it, and tightened it until it held. He did the same with the next.

When a piece resisted, he adjusted the angle and tried again. It seated without sound.

He wiped his hands on the cloth, folded it, and set it back. The box remained open. He did not close it.

He stepped away from the table and ran water over his hands to remove the dust.

evening

She was already there when he came in, sitting near the window with a book open but not held. He set what he was carrying on the counter and moved past her to wash his hands. When he finished, she had turned a page.

They occupied the room without arranging themselves around one another. He prepared food. She folded something that needed folding and set it aside. A pan heated. A chair shifted and settled again.

They ate without discussion. Plates were passed when needed. Water was poured and refilled. Neither commented on the food.

Afterward, he cleared the table while she wiped the counter. The radio came on briefly and was turned off again. She stood to stretch, then returned to her seat.

They continued in the same space, each attending to something separate. At one point she stood and crossed the room. He adjusted his position without looking up. The adjustment held.

When the light outside dimmed, neither of them responded to it.

He rinsed the glass and set it on the counter while it was still damp. The bottle was where it always was. He picked it up, tipped it once into the glass, and set it back without looking to see how much he had poured.

He carried the glass to the table and placed it near the edge, not close enough to risk a spill. He took one drink and set it down.

The light over the counter was brighter than he needed. He reached up and lowered it.

He left the glass and went to bed.

About the Author

Cameron Lane writes fiction that examines proximity, restraint, and the structures that shape human connection. His work focuses on what remains when performance falls away and presence is left to stand on its own.

He is the author of *The Squaring of a Heart* and *The Quiet One*. His novels explore the quiet negotiations that define intimacy, stability, and change.